The Perfect ghost Story?

Also available from Piccadilly Press:

The Perfect Love Story?
The Perfect Journey?
The Perfect Crime?

The Perfect Ghost Story?

Winners of The Guardian/Piccadilly writing competition for teenagers

Piccadilly Press • London

The Writing on the Wall © Lyria Eastley, 2004
Jewel Wasp © Laura Friis, 2004
Ghost's Story © Davey Heitler, 2004
The Road to Pedlington © Angharad Mead, 2004
Fear Me © Daisy Perrin, 2004
Fire House © Jenny Pritchard, 2004
Masterpiece © Liz Sutcliffe, 2004
Waking Asleep © Jonathan Tidmarsh, 2004
A Division of Myself © Rebecca Wait, 2004
Haunted Holiday © Sahra Watkin, 2004

A catalogue record for this book is available
from the British Library

ISBN: 1 85340 799 2 (trade paperback)

1 3 5 7 9 10 8 6 4 2

Printed and bound in Great Britain by Bookmarque Ltd
for the publishers Piccadilly Press Ltd,
5 Castle Road, London NW1 8PR
www.piccadillypress.co.uk

Cover photograph by Brian Cencula
Cover design by Louise Millar
Typeset by Textype Typesetters
Set in Justlefthand and Meridian

Contents

Foreword

Helen Dunmore

From ghosties and ghoulies and long-legged beasties, and things that go bump in the night, good Lord deliver us! says the old Scottish prayer. But for the three of us judging *The Perfect Ghost Story?*, the mail kept on bringing ghosts in stories that were vivid, unsettling, subtle or just plain scary.

We're all creatures of reason until the lights go out, the door begins to creak, the best friend starts to act like a stranger, or the eyes in the portrait on the wall begin to follow us around the room . . .

Joanna Carey, Cathy Hopkins and I were looking for stories which had originality, force, and above all a voice of their own which would convince readers. Every story, we hoped, would be a new door through which a reader could enter the world of the supernatural.

Each story in this collection has its own highly individual strength. It was tough to get into the top ten, and these writers deserve their success. As you read, you'll discover ghosts who feed on radioactivity, a boy haunted by his dead brother, warning words on a wall which no paint can wipe out, a house with a grim history, a diamond that can change lives, an old-fashioned bus trundling through countryside which is surely just a little too perfect to be true . . . and you'll find yourself lost in that other world of imagination and of ghosts.

The Writing on the Wall

Lyria Eastley

The Writing on the Wall

'My name's Lisa,' said the woman, handing Alice yet another copy of her book. Alice signed her name for the hundredth time that day.

'This,' continued Lisa, 'is the most haunting story I've ever read.'

'Thanks,' said Alice, 'that's what I wanted when I wrote it.'

But you didn't write it, did you? thought Alice to herself. *It came with the house. You just put it in a book, didn't you?*

Alice and her husband, Robert, had wanted an eccentric house. They tried to find something different; unique, but affordable.

They found it. They turned up on a Sunday morning to view the house. From the outside it looked small and dark, but the blue front door beckoned to them. They went to knock, but before they could, it opened. A wrinkly face peered out suspiciously. It was Mr Gill, his wife close behind. Mr and Mrs Gill were a couple with stern faces and a dislike of conversation.

The hall inside was very dark, with bare, unsanded floorboards. The living room contained only an armchair and a lamp, both coated in thick, grey dust.

Robert smiled. 'Minimalism's all the rage, I hear,' he said. His little joke fell flat on the unswept floor and crawled away to bury itself.

Despite the house being neglected, it was just what Robert and Alice had been searching for. The architecture was interesting: it seemed to consist of narrow corridors and unexpected rooms. The last room they looked at was a small, upstairs bedroom full of sunlight, but devoid of any furniture.

'This is lovely!' exclaimed Alice. 'But the estate agent said this was only a one-bedroom house . . .?'

Mrs Gill cleared her throat and said, 'Your estate agent must have been mistaken. This is the second bedroom.' Alice was surprised to hear Mrs Gill's voice; Mr Gill had done all the talking up to now.

'So whose room is this?' she asked.

'It was my daughter Sylvia's,' said Mrs Gill, not removing her gaze from Alice.

Alice smiled. 'She doesn't live here any more?'

'No,' said Mrs Gill, monotonously. 'She's dead.'

Alice felt Robert shudder next to her. She shot him a comforting glance. He smiled weakly.

That same day, they called the estate agent and put in an offer. The house was theirs.

The move was surprisingly easy. For three hours the house was alive with removal men, and it creaked and groaned as if not used to such activity. Alice decided to use the master bedroom for storage, so she and Robert would sleep in the other bedroom; her favourite room. Robert gave her a doubtful look when she mentioned this to him, but agreed once she'd given him a reassuring squeeze. That evening, they sat in their new bedroom, sharing a bottle of wine.

'I like this house a lot,' said Robert. He stood and walked around the room, humming gently. He paused. 'You know, just in the corner up there is a spot of pink paint.'

'Pardon?' said Alice.

'Up there, opposite the door, is a little blob of pink paint.'

'Well, we'll go over it when we decorate, so it's nothing to worry about.'

He continued to stare up into the left-hand corner of the room.

'Robert,' she said firmly, 'it's nothing to worry about.'

'No, I suppose not,' said Robert, and continued his ambling.

In the morning, the sunlight came streaming in through the window, giving much-needed heat to the house. Alice felt Robert roll out of bed, and she turned to say good morning.

'I think we should try to unpack what we can while it's the weekend,' she announced.

He agreed, and began searching for his clothes. He glanced up, and a puzzled look came over his face.

'Alice,' he said very slowly, 'tell me, am I mad, or has that blob of paint on the wall changed shape?'

She stumbled out of bed to look for herself. 'No, it looks just the same to me.'

'I swear it looks different.'

'It was dark last night, you just couldn't see it properly.'

Robert still looked anxious.

'Look,' said Alice, 'if it's really irritating you, we'll get one of those sample pots and paint over it, OK?'

Robert insisted they do that before they unpacked. They spent the whole day in the unfamiliar kitchen, unpacking the cardboard boxes that they'd brought from their old flat. Soon it began to feel like their home.

The time flew by. Outside the sky got darker and darker as the night swept in, and they were both unwilling to leave the sanctuary they had created, but their ascent to the bedroom soon became unavoidable. They crept up the stairs, feeling like unwelcome guests in an ancient tomb.

Robert marched into their bedroom, his patriarchal persona overriding his tomb-raider one, and switched on the light.

'The pink paint . . . it's back!'

'What?' hissed Alice.

'It's back and it says something . . . *I like* . . .'

'What?' Sure enough, the paint was back and it

was bigger. Robert started to shake.

'That doesn't look like *I like* . . . to me,' said Alice. 'Look, it's probably the old colour of the room showing through the white paint. Don't worry about it. We'll paint over it tomorrow.'

Robert glared suspiciously at it, even as he got undressed. Alice gave up and went to bed.

She heard him, muttering, 'Dead man's fingers.'

She laughed at him silently. Poor Robert was so superstitious.

When Alice woke up the next morning, Robert was already painting over the blob, his face folded in concentration. He was in a foul mood, which put Alice in a foul mood. Much of the day was spent silently vacuuming all the rooms. They ate dinner very late in the evening.

By that time, Alice could no longer stand the tension, so she announced: 'I'm going to bed, I have to get up early tomorrow.'

She could hear Robert shuffling around downstairs for some time afterwards.

She woke before the alarm. Robert was snoring gently. She didn't want to wake him, so she left the lights off as she dressed. She left the house and walked to the bus stop. Even though she had hated the old flat, at least it was only a half-hour walk from the school where she worked. She'd never had to get the bus before.

Her first class was Year Eleven, and she'd barely begun the lesson when the receptionist came in and beckoned her with a shiny fingernail. 'Your husband's on the phone, Mrs Brown,' she said sternly. This was a familiar scenario. Alice followed her to the reception area.

'Alice . . .?' Robert panted.

'Yes, Robert, what's wrong?'

'Alice, it's the writing, it's back and there's more.'

'What? Are you sure?'

'Yes, positive.'

'What does it say?

'A sentence . . . about painting the sky or something . . . I won't stay in this house alone, OK? I'm going out, I'll be back this evening.'

'OK, bye.' Alice hung up sharply and then felt guilty. Still, he was being irrational.

The receptionist smirked as Alice left. 'What was it this time, Mrs Brown? The plumbing? The neighbour's dog?' Alice did not find it funny at all.

All the staff were used to Robert's daily distress calls, but this one was different; usually his complaints were rooted in reality. But as she made her way home and the shape of the house loomed in front of her, her mind began creating gruesome pictures of terrible messages in her bedroom. She let herself into the silent house, the rational part of her mind ordering her to go into the bedroom.

There, just as Robert had said, was pink writing,

8

up in the corner of the room. It read: *I like to sit and paint the sky.*

Don't we all, thought Alice.

It was almost poetic. She went downstairs to get the stepladder.

Robert came home later in the evening.

'Did you see it? Did you see it?' he hissed. She could smell the alcohol on his breath.

'Yes, I saw it.'

'And?'

'I painted over it.'

'Yes, but what is it?'

'Writing.'

'From what?'

'I don't know, but it's not doing any harm, is it? It's probably an art project by the previous owners.'

'I do not think,' said Robert, his voice shaking, 'that the previous owners did art projects.'

'Calm down, Robert . . . Where have you been today?'

He'd been getting to know their local pubs.

All right for some, thought Alice.

The next morning she woke up before the alarm again. She left the light off, but couldn't find any socks, so she picked up a torch and started rifling. Then an urge overcame her. She turned and pointed the torch at the wall. There it was.

I like to sit and paint the sky,
I like to watch the world go by,
But my favourite thing of all
Is writing, writing on the wall.

Alice froze. Her first thought was, *What if Robert sees this?*

She'd left the stepladder and the paint in the room so she climbed up and sloshed paint on to the wall. As she did this, her mind buzzed with rational explanations. There must be a water leak somewhere, she thought. The wall's damp underneath and this old writing's showing through. Alice decided to visit the school library and find a decorating book.

At least Robert wouldn't see the writing.

Explanations swirled around in Alice's head all day, exhausting her. She didn't get time to visit the library, but the effort of the morning paid off: Robert was cheerful when she got home.

'The sentence has gone!' he shouted from upstairs as she walked through the door.

'I know, I told you, I painted over it.'

'Yes, but it's gone!'

'Yes, that's because now there are enough layers of paint to stop it showing through,' said Alice, feeling slightly irritated. At least he was happy.

'Let's go out and celebrate!' he said, charging downstairs.

They went to an expensive restaurant, and nothing, not even the bill, could bring Robert's mood down. They walked home, singing and giggling. The house was dark when they returned, but Robert marched in. Alice hung up her coat as he jogged upstairs. She heard him stride into their room. His voice drifted down, choked and shaking.

'Alice . . . Alice . . .'

She ran upstairs. The light from the hall shone through their bedroom door and formed a rectangle on the wall opposite. Robert was standing, petrified.

There, in the patch of hall light, was the writing. But there was more, and now it was all in indigo:

I like to sit and paint the sky,
I like to watch the world go by,
But my favourite thing of all
Is writing, writing on the wall.

I see the people in the street,
I know that we will never meet,
But if we did I'd tell them all
About the writing on the wall.

Wrapped up in their little lives,
Don't care much who lives or dies,
But they'd see, they'd see it all
If they saw the writing on the wall.

Alice turned to Robert, but before she could even begin to murmur a rationalisation he said, 'Alice, I will not sleep in this room.' He left, walking slowly downstairs, clutching the banister as if he were liable to fall at any moment.

Alice was spooked, but she refused to sacrifice a much-needed good night's sleep for the sake of someone's art work and some crappy paint. She stayed in the room.

The alarm woke her rudely. She drew the curtains. Light shone on to the words and she found herself thinking, *Someone poured their heart and soul into those words*. She sighed and began to get dressed. Robert was huddled up on the sofa downstairs. She didn't wake him.

Alice couldn't concentrate all day: she felt dazed and confused. She waited for Robert's call, but none came. That was almost more disturbing. She left school and jogged to the bus stop, worried sick about what kind of state he might be in.

It was already getting dark as she approached their front door and the silence was oppressive. She knocked, a heavy thudding sound. No reply. She rifled through her bag, searching for her key. Her hands shook as she unlocked the door. Robert lay in the hall, wrapped in a blanket, an empty bottle of whisky beside him. Alice propped him up.

'Alice,' he croaked, 'they don't want us here.'

'Who?' she said.

'The evil sprits . . .'

'There are no evil spirits, Robert . . . It's just . . . it's just . . .' Robert burst into weak tears. Alice put her arms around him, lost for words.

She helped him up and into the overgrown back garden, hoping that fresh air would sober him up. She sat him on the edge of the cracked patio. What else could she do?

She watched the sky turning from dark grey to dark blue, until the only light in the garden was coming from their bedroom window. Alice watched the moths dancing in it. Had Robert been up there? Suddenly, the light went out. Alice blinked into the new darkness. The light flickered back on again. Robert cringed and started whimpering. The light switched back off. Then back on. Then there was a loud smash from inside the bedroom. Alice leaped up. Robert clutched her ankle.

'No, Alice, don't go, please.'

She untangled herself and ran upstairs. When she reached the corridor, the door flung open as if she was expected.

Alice just had time to register the tornado that appeared to be in progress, before she was sucked into the room to join it. She hit the floor with a tremendous thud, smacking both her shoulder and her head hard against the floorboards. She lay, dizzy and winded, feeling a furious wind swirling above her head, and hearing her possessions smash as they were hurled against walls. Then the lights went out again.

Alice struggled to her hands and knees,

whimpering at the pain in her shoulder. She began to crawl forward, smothered by the darkness, one arm stretched blindly out, searching for something stable. She shuffled forward over debris cast aside by the force rampaging round the room. Suddenly she was bombarded by a series of hard objects. She flung herself on to her stomach, hiding her face and squealing with each hit she took.

And then silence. A deliberate calm. The eye of the storm?

She slowly lifted her head. The light was back on, but the lampshade had been torn off so the bulb glowed like a warning light. She lay at the edge of the room; like a sacrificial lamb brought to the altar of a long-forgotten civilisation.

The walls and ceiling were now covered in thin, jagged, red letters and they screamed down at her.

People often pass me by,
Their conversation is so dry,
I want to scream and tell them all:
Observe the writing on the wall.

I want you all to use your eyes
To hear my voice, to hear my cries
I want to ask you, ask you all,
WHO HAS READ THE WRITING ON THE WALL?

Just as she took this in, a vase flew past her nose and shattered against the wall. The fracas began again, and Alice started to weep softly at her powerlessness.

And then her favourite *Beatles* record hit her sharply on the ear. The sleeve was ripped, and the record scratched beyond repair. Anger spread through her like vodka. How dare this . . . thing destroy her possessions, terrorise her husband and ruin an irreplaceable record collection? She lifted her head as far off the floor as she dared. In front of her was a black marker pen. She snatched it up, climbed painfully to her feet, limped to the wall and slashed a message of her own.

I HAVE READ THE WRITING ON THE WALL

The wind stopped. The flying objects dropped to the floor. Alice stepped back and she was overcome by a wave of nausea and horror. *What am I doing?*

She limped slowly downstairs. Robert was curled up asleep on the kitchen floor. Alice crept under the blanket with him and hid in its warmth.

Alice woke late the next morning, covered in purple bruises. Had she dreamed it? Was she drunk? She cautiously made her way upstairs. Amid the chaos there was some new writing, now pale blue.

> *Back in nineteen-sixty-three,*
> *My own life was taken by me,*
> *I need to tell you, tell you all,*
> *About the writing on the wall.*

It was signed, *Sylvia Gill.*

Alice considered this. She picked up a notepad and

pen from the floor, and began to copy the writing.

She went down to the living room and sat at the table. She looked at the notebook. Then she wrote a sentence, then another. Soon the notepad was filled with writing.

Some time later she heard a shuffling in the hall; it was Robert. He was standing at the bottom of the stairs, staring up intently.

'Robert,' said Alice, gently, 'it's OK. You can go up.'

He looked nervous. Alice gave him her reassuring smile. 'I'll go with you,' she said.

She led him upstairs and into the room. The writing was gone.

His face lit up with relief, he turned and embraced her eagerly, then noticed the notebook.

'It's the story,' said Alice.

'Make it out to Michael, please.'

Alice signed the book automatically.

She looked at where she'd written her name and blinked. There, written in pink ink: *Sylvia Gill* . . .

Jewel Wasp

Laura Friis

Jewel Wasp

'Joel's right. Free will is arguably the most important thing we have, it's what makes us human. All our decisions are based on the assumption that we have the freedom to choose what actions we take. But if this freedom is an illusion, what are the implications? Ama?'

Miss Keane paused, and the name shook Cam out of his reverie. He yawned as if he was waking from a long sleep, and stretched unobtrusively. Nevertheless, Miss Keane noticed.

'Am I boring you, Mr Sugden? Perhaps you could treat us to a more interesting comment on the illusion of free will?'

Cam could feel them smirking all around him. He had been a million miles away – the effect school usually had on him – and had no idea what they had been talking about. He looked involuntarily at Ama Khan, who looked back gravely, but wasn't laughing at him. He felt his face turn a fiery red and stared down at the desk, glad that he always sat at the back. Miss Keane was merciful.

'Good to know I can keep my job for now . . . sorry, Ama?'

Ama spoke diffidently, but not reluctantly. 'I was going to say that it has implications for the traditional image of God, because if God really is omnipotent and benevolent, he wouldn't deceive us into thinking we had free will.'

'Well, that depends on the tradition,' Keane said. 'The traditional Christian view of God is certainly of a perfect being, but look at the Greeks. Look at Zeus. He lies, tricks, cheats on his wife . . .'

Cam tuned out again. He was interested in Ama, not free will, and certainly not the ancient Greeks. He scratched a hole in his file paper with a sharp pencil, and then clicked his pen for the remaining ten minutes of the lesson. It was a soul-destroying occupation, but easily more interesting than one of Keane's deep philosophical tangents. She was a good teacher, but Cam reckoned life was for living, not thinking about. He planned to get round to living it sometime soon.

Cam longed for excitement, or perhaps it was more that he longed to be exciting. He yearned to be somebody people wondered about, an alluring enigma. The kind of person who had no self-doubt. Whereas Cam was rarely sure about anything.

Ama, for instance. Ama would see through his thin veneer of confidence within seconds, if they ever got as far as a conversation. She smiled as they left the classroom, and opened her mouth slightly as if she would speak to him – something he had silently dreamed of for months – but instead of an answering smile, instead of a witty, conversational gambit, he looked hard at the floor and rushed past her into the corridor, out to the grounds.

He walked home alone, as his friends were at various after-school clubs. Cam would have been happy to achieve fame – even notoriety – in music, sport or debate, but he had no shining talents. He didn't want to waste his time. The one thing he wasn't going to let himself be was mediocre. He had little hope of being able to explain this to his father.

'I've seen Mr Demarco, and I've told him I'm stopping violin lessons,' Cam announced at the supper table. His father never appreciated dissemblers; perhaps the direct approach would keep him calmer.

'Oh, that's good – you *what*?'

Or perhaps not.

Dad always overreacts, Cam thought, barely able to hear himself think over his father's lecture. The only person who seemed unaffected by the atmosphere was his mum, who didn't once lift her eyes from the book she was reading. Cam wondered if his father noticed that she never turned a page.

'I don't understand you,' his father declared. 'I don't want to make you into a Mozart, Cam, I just think you should make an effort to learn some new skills.'

'It's not a *skill*,' Cam cried, goaded. 'Either you can play or you can't. I don't want to be one of those people who think they're achieving something just because they can ape something really good.'

He hated the scornful expression that spread slowly over his father's face. He had the feeling that it had always been there underneath, and would have emerged whatever he had said.

'What a pompous thing to say. You really think a lot of yourself, don't you?'

Cam couldn't bear to be so completely misunderstood. He shouted something, he wasn't sure what, then pushed back his chair and stormed upstairs.

'Did Mozart play the violin?' his mother asked his father as he left. His dad snorted.

In his room Cam threw a few shoes at the wall. The obvious impotence of his anger was embarrassing, even in his solitude. *If Ama could see you now*, he thought.

After an hour or so he had calmed down enough to feel terrible. His father – ugly, sandy-bearded, mean-minded git that he was – might be right, though Cam hated to even consider it. Had he truly been arrogant? He just didn't want a *hobby*. He had quit because he knew the awkward scrapings of the violin he produced were nothing like the wild, lonely beauty it was meant to call up. Even the instrument itself seemed to look sideways at him when he played.

But now that he knew he never had to play it again, contrarily he longed to. And he wanted to show his father that he wasn't the conceited brat he had been taken for. But Demarco would laugh in his face if he changed his mind again. And he would have to climb all those stairs to the music office, knock on the door, wait to be invited in, then speak – his throat blocked as he thought of it. He didn't know what to do.

Almost involuntarily – he was never sure afterwards whether he had been compelled to – he turned to his big wooden chest, which was padlocked.

'My dad says it's all in the subconscious,' Luke had said with false confidence the night after his party. 'The little muscles in your hand move without you realising, so really you're just answering your own questions.'

He didn't know why he kept this thing locked away. It was made of diamond, and valuable, but that wasn't why. He just felt it wouldn't be wise to have it out where he would look at it every day.

It was in an envelope, under a rumpled comic strip he and Marks had begun when they were nine, and never finished.

'I knew it was a load of bollocks,' Benson had said without conviction.

'It was a laugh, anyway,' Marks had said with a shrug, and gladly they had talked of something else.

They had wanted to believe it, Cam thought. What would the world be like if there were *things* out there, things that would talk to you?

It hung on a silky silver chain, a conical diamond weight sparkling in the light, the facets making it impossible to see the centre. Fire clouded his vision momentarily, blinding as tears. He blinked, and it was gone.

'Is my name Roger?' he asked it. It swung right. No.

'Is my name Cam?' he asked. It swung away from him. Yes.

'Can I play the violin?' he asked. It swung right. He laughed.

'Maybe you aren't bollocks after all,' he told it. 'Huh?'

I'm talking to a pendulum, he thought. *This can't be good.*

Still, he felt better. He played with it all evening, not getting bored. It knew things a chunk of diamond could never know. It didn't feel like he was talking to a rock, it felt like there was someone in the room with him. Finally he decided to ask it something he really wanted to know.

'Does Ama like me?'

It twinkled a cheerful yes.

'Should I ask her out?'

It didn't move at all. He shook it, and it twirled under his hand in what he thought of as an aggrieved way.

'Sorry,' he said, then shook his head in disgust. Why was he apologising? There was no little green leprechaun living in the diamond. He put it back in the envelope and on the table with his lamp, and went to bed.

He dreamed. In the night he woke up, worried about Demarco and what he would say. Barely even realising what he was doing – it would never have occurred to him normally – he reached out for the pendulum by his bed, and shook it out into his hand.

'Should I talk to Demarco?' he whispered. The bedroom was dark, but he could see the pendulum quite clearly. It was luminous, but not in a tacky glow-in-the-dark way. It was like it was lit from the inside. It threw a warm light on to his bedcovers. Half-asleep, half-awake, this didn't strike him as strange. He repeated his question, blinking.

Yes, it said. Cam could almost hear it speak as it glided through the air, suspended gracefully on its chain. The voice was husky, ruminative.

'But he'll *crucify* me,' Cam whimpered. It swung its yes more firmly, although he got the distinct impression it didn't like his choice of words. Spooked, he wanted to shove it in his sock drawer, but it didn't feel right. He laid it carefully back on the table, and fell into a dark, weighty sleep.

Next morning, the pendulum was back in the envelope, ready to go hidden to school. He didn't want anyone to see it and ask questions, as he hated having to explain himself. His growing belief in the diamond's powers was not something he wanted to talk about. It was too strange, too personal.

His dad gave him a lift, both of them gritty-eyed and silent. Cam sat in the back. They listened to Terry

Wogan – his father's choice. He walked across the crowded school drive and found Marks in the library. They both arrived early, and always hung out there before registration.

'Why did you give me the pendulum?' Cam asked with forced casualness, after they had talked about what now seemed like unimportant things for half an hour.

'The what?' Marks asked, looking uneasy. Cam knew he had heard.

'The thing we tried out at Luke's party.'

'Oh, that.' Marks lowered his voice, as if they were in a church. 'Well, it was rubbish, wasn't it? Why let a glorified necklace make decisions for you? And . . . hell . . . know it sounds stupid, but I kept having really weird dreams when it was in my room. Then, when I got rid of it they stopped.'

'What kind of dreams?'

'Just – weird ones.'

Cam's fingers closed around the cold diamond in his pocket.

He waited outside Demarco's office at break, tilting the diamond to and from the light until he was bored, but couldn't drag his eyes away. When Demarco called him inside he wasn't ready. His palms were damp and tingling. He knew Demarco would make him feel indecisive, childish, stupid. And why was he here at all? Because the pendulum had told him to be. He really was going crazy.

'Mr Sugden,' Demarco said. Cam frowned. Demarco sounded as brisk as always, but almost pleasant.

'Could I – I mean I want to – I've –' he stammered.

'Changed your mind? I thought you might. Shall I put you back down for the Thursday slot?'

Dazed, Cam nodded. Outside the door again, he couldn't believe it. Demarco was famous for his caustic tongue, and hated to be messed around. He should have made mincemeat out of Cam, but instead he had been *nice*. Cam took the pendulum from his pocket, spilling the silver into his hand thoughtfully.

'Sorry for doubting you,' he said, half-serious, half-joking.

It gleamed.

School sucked, but Cam found that with the pendulum in his hand it didn't suck so much. He used it to get full marks on his geography multiple-choice test, which he hadn't revised for, and to see whether there were any hot dogs left in the canteen without having to join the queue.

'You must be psychic,' Benson said, coming back to the lunch table without hot dogs, and breathless from the crush. Cam smiled.

'Pay up,' he said. Benson and Luke flicked fifty pence coins across the table.

'Cheapskate,' Luke said.

'No I'm not. I can get more chips with this.'

'Or you could come to the snooker club,' Luke suggested. 'Tonight, after school?'

Cam wanted to say yes, but he couldn't. Not without checking. He physically couldn't get the words out. His fists clenched.

'Just a second,' he said, and ducked under the table, pretending to get something out of his bag. Instead, he steadied his shaking hands, and asked the pendulum. It swerved an emphatic no.

'I can't tonight,' he said.

When school finished he watched them leave together, with a strange mixture of feelings. He wanted badly to be with them, but thinking that made him feel a pang of disloyalty, to whom he wasn't sure. It *couldn't* be the pendulum. He hung round by the school gates, waiting for the late bus.

'You look cheerful,' said a girl, laughing behind him.

He turned round, ready to snarl, then he saw it was Ama and a grin split his face. With the pendulum clutched in his hand he didn't feel so shy.

'Just bored,' he said.

'Talk to me, then. I'm bored too,' she said.

It was a lot easier than he expected, except that the one thing that was constantly on his mind he couldn't talk about. He saw her eyes move to his closed hand every so often, and wanted to share the excitement his new skill gave him – and perhaps that he was a little afraid of it, too.

Should I tell her? he thought.

The pendulum lurched in his hand. Without needing to see the movement he knew that it was

telling him no. It had been right about the snooker –
if he had gone he would never have met Ama, but
now he wanted to go against it, and it wouldn't let
him. It had a will independent of his own . . .
stronger than his own?

That was unthinkable.

'Do you want to go for coffee tomorrow?' he
blurted – anything to distract himself, then went red.

'I'd love to,' Ama said.

His dreams that night were terrible, ceaseless and
disjointed. In every one he was trying to contain a
monster – a lion in a cage, next door's murderous
Alsatian in their garden, a nameless snarling thing in
his bedroom cupboard. He knew that if any one of
them got out they would rip him to rags. He was
losing strength and will when he woke. There was
none of the relief that waking from a bad dream
usually brings; if anything, he felt worse. Somehow,
the overcast nightmare atmosphere had come with
him into life.

Coffee with Ama had to go well. If he clammed up
she would probably never speak to him again, or
worse, only out of pity. He couldn't decide what to
wear. He thought the brown shirt, the pendulum
thought the blue one. He wore the brown one anyway,
and shoved the pendulum viciously into his pocket.

'Stupid lump of rock,' he muttered. 'What the hell
do you know?'

He felt its determination – *malice* – all the way up the road, and by the time he got to the bus stop he couldn't take it any more. He went home and changed into the blue shirt. He didn't like it nearly as much, but he didn't have a choice.

No choice? How far would you go to do what the diamond says?

It made him late. He was sweating, nervous about Ama and now unashamedly scared of the pendulum, or what was inside it.

'Sorry, the bus was late,' he lied, sliding into his seat. Ama shrugged, a motion that was accepting rather than dismissive. She looked amazing, her hair midnight black against the blue she was wearing, but he barely noticed. All his efforts were concentrated on staying normal and light-hearted, and trying not to choke on the panic that bubbled under the ripple of his conversation. He appeared more confident than he had ever been. They talked about school, parents. He made her laugh. He confided that he was scared of Demarco, and hated Keane because she made him feel stupid.

' "Treat us to a more interesting comment on the illusion of free will, Mr Sugden?" ' Ama quoted. Cam froze. She flushed, thinking she had said something tactless.

'I remember what teachers say,' she said, stirring her coffee. 'It's a quirk of mine. Good for exams, though.'

'She says free will is the most important thing we

have,' Cam remembered slowly. It was as if he wasn't talking to Ama any more.

'Oh, you shouldn't listen to Keane. She just likes the sound of her own voice.'

'I – I have to get home,' Cam said. 'See you on Monday.'

He didn't wait for her reply but took the stairs two at a time and rushed out into the street. He thought he was going to be sick, but out in the cold air he hardly felt anything any more. Instead he started running, ran until he was out of breath and he no longer recognised the streets he was passing through. He stopped. It was difficult to think. All he was conscious of was the pendulum, its thoughts, its will in him.

He flinched from the heat of searing fire when he touched it, saw the flickering red of flame always in the back of his mind. He heard the roar, the spit of it, and felt an overwhelming temptation to lie down on the pavement and be consumed; stop fighting. Instead he walked to the curb and held it at arm's length over the storm drain.

What makes us human, he thought desperately. But he couldn't drop it.

His struggles must have been horrible to watch, like a fly in a web – everyone knows it will die. Like a fly, he was trapped – the spider was stronger than he was, and there was no way out. The pendulum had caught him.

He clutched it close to him and felt it become

lighter, a broken vessel, a shed skin. He felt his eyes bulge and his throat constrict, and something intangible give inside. Then emptiness, darkness.

Slowly, Cam Sugden's body stood up, the shattered diamond falling from its open fist, and walked away with a new will.

Ghost's Story

Davey Heitler

Ghost's Story

The sun sets across a barren landscape, pock-marked by craters and the rubble of a desolate city. A small girl is skipping through the ruins, heading for the big hill. What is unusual about this is that the girl is literally skipping *through* the ruins, not around them, as is common practice. There is also a slight transparency about her, a certain greyness even. She is singing softly to herself.

This, despite all appearances, is not a story about ghosts. This is a story about humans. This is the story that poltergeist children are told if they won't eat their radioactive greens. This is the story ghosts tell around hushed campfires, the story that makes many of the oldest spectres fall silent and leave the room. This is the story adolescent ghosts laugh at, showing they don't believe in humans. However, as with most stories of its type, it has a habit of seeming more real than reality should allow.

As the last sliver of light fades from view behind the horizon, little stars pop into life and twinkle in the clear night sky. A shooting star whizzes overhead and crashes on top of the hill overlooking the city. A small explosion echoes in the valley, then all is eerily silent.

* * *

As part of every young ghost's education, they are told about the birthday of the world. The world was born two hundred and fifty-eight years ago, and was designed as a paradise for ghosts. Before the birth, there was only light. Then God spoke: 'Let there be darkness!' And lo, there was darkness. And with the darkness came the Chosen. For God, in his infinite wisdom, had created the Chosen People, the Blessed Ones. According to the legend, although nobody really believes legends, he had also created the humans not long after. Fortunately, the religious ghosts always seemed to find a way to sidestep this part of creation.

Maybe God was just having a bad night.

The silence of the dark is pierced by a terrified scream.

And as a homeland for the Chosen, God created the Promised Land – Hiroshima it was called, and it was a paradise. The humans, if they existed, dared not venture near, and the Chosen had a supply of radiation so vast it would never run out. Or so they had thought. After many long years the supply began to dwindle, and the Chosen grew hungry.

'It's horrible!' screamed Emma as she raced down the ruined street. Many bleary-eyed ghosts peered up from the ground, most of them having only just woken, to stare with bewilderment at the girl. She skidded round the corner at a speed that would have made a spectral cheetah blink, and rushed through the door to her home. Any non-ghost would have noticed that she didn't bother to open it first, but then there weren't any non-ghosts in Hiroshima.

'Mum! Mum!' she screamed at the top of her voice. An older female ghost floated up through the floorboards of the ruined building, and rushed to the wailing Emma. Any hope of maternal comforting quickly passed from Emma's mind, however, as her mother glared at her fiercely. Mistress Frayne, as she was known by those who weren't close to her (and there weren't any ghosts who dared to consider themselves close enough to Mistress Frayne to call her anything else), had a stare that could punch through a brick wall. Quite a feat, as the Chosen were incorporeal. Emma braced herself.

'Emma Rosemary Frayne, what *have* you been doing?'

The year is 2203, precisely two hundred and fifty-eight years since the war that destroyed the world. At least the world that people were used to. Humans all but wiped themselves out in a nuclear holocaust that left Earth unable to sustain life. The handful of survivors fled into space, the levels of radiation on the surface being too high for any living thing to survive. Those few survivors sought refuge on giant space stations, and there they monitored Earth, knowing that although it may take thousands of years, some day they would go home.

* * *

'But mum, I saw it, honest I did!' Emma protested as her mother pushed her below ground. They floated through the sodden earth for a few metres before passing through a metal plate and arriving at . . . Ghost homes are made out of a special metal called epsion. Tainted by radiation, it was the only material, apart from ectoplasm, that ghosts were able to touch, and thus was perfect building material. In order to protect them from the sun, the Chosen had used epsion to hollow out great underground caves. It was in these holes that the ghosts proceeded to build their homes.

The Frayne home was not particularly large, but it was very comfortable. There were three rooms, as with most ghost homes; the sleeping room (ghosts have no need of beds), the lounge (which also included a dining table), and the bathroom. The bathroom contained only a shower, with hot and cold running ectoplasm. Actually, ectoplasm doesn't run, it sort of oozes, but it feels wrong saying hot and cold *oozing* ectoplasm.

'Mum!' whined Emma as she was ushered into the sleeping room. 'It was there, honest!' She tried one last pleading whimper, before her mother slammed the door behind her.

Mrs Frayne sighed. This was merely for the look of the thing, as ghosts don't breathe air, but some habits have the tenacity to follow you into the afterlife (or as the ghosts call it, the newlife). She should never have let Emma stay up late that time and listen to Old Man Fergus's human stories. Emma had been having daymares for a while now, so this story wasn't entirely unexpected. Humans indeed! Still, there was something about the way she had looked, the way she spoke, that left a tiny twinkle of doubt in Mrs Frayne's otherwise brick-wall of a mind. (It wasn't that Mrs Frayne wasn't open to new ideas; it was just that new ideas seemed to politely avoid her.)

As the radiation levels on Earth began to dwindle more rapidly than scientists had predicted, the survivors began to prepare for the day of their homecoming. Landing modules were built, technology was developed, people were trained in how to adapt to life on the earth's surface. An air of excitement gripped them, and few noticed that the radiation was decreasing at a rate far in excess of anyone's predictions. Sure, a few observant scientists came out with ludicrous theories that a species had evolved to use the radiation as a food source, but nobody believed them. As is so often the case with discoveries that people don't want to be true, they were swept under the carpet; the people behind them locked away in asylums. As is also so often the case, people didn't find out how right these lunatics were until much later.

For the second time that night, the silence was split by a terrified scream.

When something spooks a ghost, there will usually be a gathering to ascertain what the problem is and what can be done about it. Something had obviously rattled Mrs Frayne, and she wasn't the sort for whom rattled was normally an option. The ghosts met in the ruined husk of a once-great library, which held in its heyday thousands upon thousands of books. Time and a nuclear holocaust had not been kind to the library, and now all the countless pages of accumulated knowledge were just so much dust and ash. The ghosts had always looked on the library as a sort of town hall, and once the word had gone out that something had freaked Mrs Frayne, everyone gathered there.

'Say what you like, I saw what I saw. And what's more what I saw was *real*.'

The collected ghosts looked embarrassed. Eventually, one, an older-looking ghost, opened his mouth to speak. Before he could utter a word, Mrs Frayne cut in with an angry glare.

'Yes, I *am* feeling all right.'

The ghost deflated slightly. He then opened his mouth again, to much the same result.

'No, I didn't imagine it, it was there, a human, an actual human!'

Hushed whispers rippled through the crowd.

'A human?'

'Impossible.'

'She must be seeing things.'

The older ghost was Old Man Fergus. (His name was Fergus, he was an old man, and he lacked any imagination.) Although ghosts didn't have leaders, he was almost a father figure for the ghost community.

'All right, Mistress Frayne. Show us.'

The wind picked up and began to whistle and howl in the rubble of the city. Moving completely silently, appearing for all the world like a floating mist, the ghosts made their way up the side of the hill. When they cleared the top of the rise they looked down – on the smouldering remains of the *Shogun*.

Jeff woke up. He immediately wished he hadn't bothered. The memories of the past few hours flitted back to him, through the murky quagmires of his short-term memory. The hero's farewell (similar in many ways to a hero's welcome, but going in the other direction), the approach on Earth, the beginning stages of re-entry, the . . . And then what? He couldn't remember. An alarm had gone off, somebody had screamed (probably himself), and then nothing. Blackness. It sat there, a gaping hole in his memory, mocking him.

He opened his eyes. He could see a black sky, with thousands of stars twinkling down on him in fake concern. He turned his head slightly to the left, ignoring the searing pain, to look on the shattered remains of his ship. Blast, so much for the hero's return. With infinite sluggishness he turned again, this time to look at a group of wide-eyed ghosts. There was a second's pause which seemed to last a millennium, and then, as a body, the ghosts turned and ran, screaming as they did so. All that is, except one.

'So, you're real, then.'

Jeff didn't know how to respond. It was very rare for people to question his existence, especially when they were little girls who were, shall we say, disadvantaged in the solidness department. For some reason that he could not explain, he felt an explanation was required.

'Uh . . . Yeah. I'm real. Yes. Er . . . My ship crashed. Over there. Yes.'

Nothing from the girl, just that same curious stare. It was beginning to unnerve him. Eventually, after studying him with her head at a slight angle, she spoke.

'You startled me before. I didn't think humans were real. I don't usually lose my grip like that, honest. I'm usually very practical and sensible.'

Out of the corner of his eye, Jeff saw that several of the more brave ghosts had returned, and were peeping over rocks with wide eyes.

'Are you listening to me?'

Jeff blinked. No, she was still there, that ghost girl. He couldn't think of anything to say, so he just smiled in an attempt to appease her. The other ghosts were talking in hushed voices, and it seemed they were discussing him. He craned his neck to hear, but the wind carried their voices away before he could catch them. Resigned to his state of paralysis, he lay there, trying to ignore the little girl's continuing scrutiny.

After a few minutes the gathered ghosts appeared to reach a consensus. One of the older ones walked towards him, a green glowing rod of metal in his transparent hands. The other ghosts cheered him on with words of encouragement from behind the safety of a large rock.

'Uh, hi, my name is Jeff. Who are –' said Jeff, as the ghost raised the glowing bar and hit him on the head.

Jeff awoke once again, this time with the feeling that there was a man trapped inside his head, trying to make an escape using a heavy mallet. As he tried to re-gather his thoughts, a bright light was flashed in his eyes.

'Hey, this one's alive!' cried a distinctly human voice.

Jeff felt strong, tangible hands lift him up. There were several men around, and there was the rushing sound of a parked ship's engine. He was being rescued!

'Wow, you're hooching with radiation. I'm surprised you aren't glowing!' The owner of the voice helped him along the charred ground towards the welcoming door of the ship, a bright light that beckoned him. As he stumbled on board he took one last look at the ruined city. Although it might have just been a trick of the light, he thought he could see a greyish mist, slowly making its way up into the air, heading for space. Then the door was closed, and he was gone, blasting off to his hero's return. Yay! Cue cheering crowds and flying confetti!

When Jeff returned to the space station, he had to be given immediate radiation treatment to recover. What the scientists didn't know was that the radiation in him had been from the rod of epsion the ghost had hit him with. Jeff thought it best to remain quiet about that, as people who talk about ghosts hitting you on the head very rarely received pay rises. The humans would have to wait for their homecoming.

The ghosts, having realised that humans really did exist, and because of the dwindling amount of radiation on Earth, decided to leave and seek out a new home amongst the stars.

Earth was empty. God first created the Chosen, and then the humans. Tough act to follow, but God has had a lot of practice.

The Road to Pedlington

Angharad Mead

The Road to Pedlington

The train drew slowly into the station with a resounding sigh from the axles, and a hiss of steam escaping from the ancient pistons. It was the only steam locomotive to operate on this particular stretch of railway, and was beginning to feel the inevitable strain of sixty years' loyal service. Rosemary, always fascinated by anything to do with the past, had spent most of her journey running her hands over the fading cover of the seat beside her and wondering what sort of people might have sat there, and what they might have been thinking as undulating landscapes and brief glimpses of rural communities flashed past the windows. Now, however, she was more concerned with gathering her belongings and leaving the simple comfort of the train in order to battle against the elements.

Standing alone and bedraggled on the platform five minutes later, Rosemary cast her eyes around for a porter, ticket vendor or even fellow passenger – anyone whom she could ask about a taxi. There was nobody to be seen; she was obviously the only person to have alighted there, and the station was unmanned. She looked wearily down at the two battered suitcases and the heavy black cello case which comprised her luggage. It was an awful lot to carry seven kilometres.

Nevertheless, there seemed to be no other plausible way of reaching the village, so reluctantly she swung the cello over her shoulder and took a decrepit suitcase in each hand, struggling with the uneven weight. She made it as far as the road, which was actually a muddy bridle track posing as a road, and then realised the ridiculousness of her situation. There had to be some way she could find a cab, and the sooner the better; a sharp sting on the cheek informed her that the rain was transforming into malicious hailstones.

Rosemary was just putting down her bags to look for her mobile phone when a bus rounded the corner. It was an old bus, painted a charming green and warm cream, but the paint was flaking down the sides, and the windows could have used a good clean. The driver, obviously recognising Rosemary's plight, slowed down until he was level with her.

'Do you need to go into the village?' he asked, smiling in a friendly way which, Rosemary reflected, you hardly ever saw in the city these days.

'Yes, please,' she said, hardly believing her luck, and proceeded to load both herself and her luggage on to the bus after a brief struggle with the cello, which at first refused flatly to go through the door. 'Thank you very much for stopping,' she said to the driver.

'You're welcome,' he told her, and the bus revved into life once more.

Rosemary made her way to a seat in the middle of

the bus and gladly set her heavy suitcases down on the floor by her feet. The bus wasn't crowded but there were a fair amount of people, who were all looking at her with extreme interest, probably because of the cello, which was dominating two seats all of its own. There was something odd about the people which Rosemary couldn't quite put her finger on; something about the way they dressed – she felt a little out of place in her old jeans and brightly-coloured sweatshirt. Still, they didn't seem at all put off by her attire, and she soon began to relax as friendly conversation began.

'Have you been to the village before?' asked a rosy-cheeked woman, who was carrying a basket of freshly harvested apples. She offered one to Rosemary, who declined, although they certainly looked appetising. 'You'll love it there, it's a wonderful place.' Several people around them nodded in agreement. Rosemary found herself warming towards these travellers, and was glad she'd found the bus – or rather the bus had found her – instead of an impersonal minicab.

'Excuse me,' said a timid-looking man at the back of the bus. 'Forgive me if I'm wrong, but . . . is that a cello? Goodness, it's big, it must be a beautiful object.'

Rosemary nodded. She liked it when people took an interest in her instrument, and when people paid it compliments it was as if they were complimenting her.

'I used to play the cello,' the man at the back

continued, sinking into a reverie, 'used to play at village barn dances.' He smiled at this recollection, but there was melancholy rooted in his eyes. Rosemary longed to ask why he no longer played, but decided not to, as she'd only just met him.

'When you're in the village,' said a small, hunched man at the very front of the bus, 'do look in on the church. Remarkable architecture.'

Rosemary could see from his clerical dog-collar that he was a vicar, and from the expression on his face she could tell that he was very proud of his church and of his parish.

'I'd love to go and see it,' she assured him, and he looked as pleased as she had done when her cello was complimented. It was strange, she thought to herself, the way people could become so attached to objects, or places or buildings. Her cello was a part of her, and she had no doubt that the village church was a part of the vicar in the same way.

Everyone was being so friendly that Rosemary felt embarrassed at having so little to say in return. She gazed out of the window beside her at the heather-armoured hillside, which led her eye down into a deep, shadowy ravine. At the bottom stood some yew trees, sombrely guarding the rocky terrain, and watching gravely as a small stream played merrily at their feet.

'It's beautiful countryside,' said Rosemary.

A hush had spread over the travellers on the bus. A few nodded, one or two gazed thoughtfully at the yew trees, somehow preoccupied. The woman with the basket of apples eventually broke the silence.

'It's true, it is beautiful, but the ravine is a devilish place for accidents, especially if the road is slippery.'

The bus moved on, and the rocky hillside gave way to rich fields, dotted here and there with white, peaceful forms, which Rosemary could just make out to be sheep. She noticed – as she gazed out of the window – that the hail had stopped, and a sunbeam the colour of old-fashioned lemon bonbons was reaching out to kiss the wet grass. She was so entranced by the beauty of the landscape that she hardly heard the cellist speak, and she had to spin round to avoid appearing impolite.

'Are you staying with friends in the village?' he enquired, absently biting into an apple offered to him by the rosy-cheeked woman, who again offered one to Rosemary. This time she accepted, and bit into it with a satisfying crunch, savouring the taste of the sweet but tantalisingly sharp juice.

'Actually, I'm going to stay with my aunt,' she told them. 'She recently moved into the village from London, and now that she's so far away she doesn't get very many relatives visiting her. You might know her house; it's called The Gables.'

'The Gables!' exclaimed the rosy-cheeked woman and the cellist in unison. 'Why,' continued the latter, 'it's right opposite my cottage! But I can't say I know your aunt.'

This didn't surprise Rosemary one bit; her aunt had never been the most sociable of people, and having lived in the village for a mere three weeks had probably not got very well-acquainted with any of the residents yet.

'Well,' she said, glad that she'd made some friends in the village before she'd even got there, 'maybe I can pop in to see you before I leave for London again.'

The man smiled gently. 'Yes,' he said. 'Maybe.'

After a short period of time the clatter of bus wheels on cobbles announced their arrival in the village. The sun had now come out fully from behind the gauzy network of clouds, and Rosemary was delighted to have pleasant weather to welcome her. As the bus drew to a halt beside the village green she got up, collected her suitcases and cello, and slowly made her way up front to the driver.

'What do I owe you?' she asked, fumbling for her purse.

'It doesn't matter,' he said with a friendly wink. 'We were passing through anyway.'

Rosemary stepped off the bus and on to the cobbled road. As she looked around she heard the engine choke into life, and the bus drive away slowly into the distance. 'You're right,' she began, turning around to address her travelling companions, 'It *is* beautiful . . .' But there was no one there. They had obviously all remained on the bus.

A surge of panic washed over Rosemary; what if

this wasn't the right village? But no, there was the pub with its hand-painted sign, declaring, The Fox and Goose Inn, just as her aunt had described it to her. Oh well, maybe they had gone to do some shopping in a town nearby – she'd ask them tomorrow.

Lugging the two big suitcases and the cello case she started off down the nearest street, which, with the second piece of luck that day, turned out to be her aunt's. The Gables was a pretty little house, with a tangled but charming rose creeper growing over the doorway and a fountain happily tinkling away on the neatly-trimmed lawn. Rosemary rang the doorbell, wondering if she could possibly have had a better afternoon – the sun was out, she'd had a pleasant journey, and now here she was in a village that seemed an idyll of rustic charm.

'Rosemary!' Her aunt opened the door only a second or two after the bell had been rung, genuinely elated to see her niece. 'Did you have a pleasant journey down? I've made up the guest room for you. Leave the cello down here, that's it, we'll take up a suitcase each. This way . . .' She led the way up a twisting, narrow flight of stairs that eventually reached a small landing. Rosemary's room was directly off this landing, and had a window, which looked out on to the quiet little street below.

'Well,' said her aunt, setting down the suitcase and surveying the room with a critical eye to make sure it was perfect for her niece, 'how do you like it?'

'It's lovely, thank you,' said Rosemary, taking in the neat white bed with the lacy bedspread and the wallpaper with its cheerful floral design. 'What a sweet room.'

'Yes, I think so,' said her aunt. 'But I particularly thought you'd like the view.'

Rosemary wandered over to the little window to take a look. She'd probably be able to see the cellist's house – he'd said he lived opposite The Gables.

She pulled back the pale, sugary-pink curtain, expecting to see a row of neat little cottages. Instead there was a row of small craft shops, sweet little buildings whose window boxes overflowed with torrents of brightly-coloured pansies, but shops nonetheless.

'There,' said her aunt with a smile, 'I thought the shops would make you feel at home.'

Rosemary was confused. 'But the man I met on the bus said that he had a cottage opposite your house. I remember clearly . . .'

Now it was her aunt's turn to look confused. 'Bus? I assumed you came here in a taxi. What are you talking about? There aren't any bus services to this village.'

'I definitely came on a bus.'

At that moment there came a crashing sound and a rather homely-looking woman appeared in the doorway. Rosemary assumed that this was the housekeeper her aunt had talked about.

'I'm terribly sorry, miss,' she said, and Rosemary

half-expected her to curtsey like a servant from an old black-and-white film, 'but I just tripped over your instrument. I hope I haven't broken it.'

'I wouldn't worry,' Rosemary reassured her, having done the same thing herself, a number of times. 'It's very robust.' The housekeeper looked immensely relieved, and turned to bustle back downstairs again.

'One other thing,' said Rosemary's aunt, and the woman halted in the doorway. 'Rosemary says she came by bus – I couldn't find one the other day. Where do they stop?'

The housekeeper looked puzzled. 'There aren't any buses,' she said. 'There haven't been buses to this village for . . . let me see . . . just over twenty years now. Not since there was an horrific accident. One day, the village bus was taking a group of passengers along the road to Pedlington, you know, towards the station, and the bus just lost control and careered into the ravine. Terribly sad. Everyone was killed. And such nice people they were too. There was the Reverend Thatcher, and Mr Cunningham, the local musician – played a cello like yours, I believe – and Mrs Barnham, who made her own cider, and of course the driver . . . anyway, there hasn't been a bus service since.'

Rosemary stood still, drinking in this information. 'Where did this happen?' she asked, but she already knew.

'Along the stretch of road just before the sheep farms. Near the big yew trees.'

'Rosemary, are you all right?' her aunt asked.

But Rosemary wasn't listening. She was gazing out at the stretch of road which snaked off away from the village towards the horizon. She wasn't sure, it might have been a smut on the glass, or an illusion in the fading light, but she thought that she could see the outline of a little green and cream bus, growing smaller and smaller as it drove off into the distance.

Fear Me

Daisy Perrin

Fear Me

Over the past few years, I have come to realise that working in an office in Soho can be extraordinarily interesting. Often, I've found that even the most recent discoveries can wing their way to Soho in a matter of minutes. Of course, it's not all newspapers, armchairs and smoking pipes. You have to work hard in this office. If you don't, people know, and I'm not just talking about live people.

'Ghostbusters' is a commonly-used term to describe the workers at Bridge and Jay Ltd. Personally, I prefer to call myself a detective. It introduces more of a mysterious element to the job, which of course is true. In fact, in my time at Bridge and Jay, I have discovered and dealt with sixteen regular ghosts, three poltergeists and a ghoul. All of these cases have been simple compared to my most recent assignment, which I was given in late September last year. This one sticks out the most, and not in a pleasant way.

I was not expecting my first client on Monday morning. I had only really gone into work to clear away the paperwork from the previous week. Nevertheless, I agreed to see her and help her with her problem. My secretary, Pete Feathercon, handed me the typed brief as I arrived.

'Katherine Waters?' I enquired, reading the name at the top of the sheet.

'Yes, Mr Parker,' Pete answered, shuffling his feet restlessly under his desk. 'She claims to have a ghost problem.'

'Show her in,' I replied, absent-mindedly placing my briefcase in the waste-paper bin. Miss Waters entered as I was retrieving it.

'Noel Parker?' she asked, quietly. I could see from her appearance that she was tired. Her brown hair was matted and fell in a tangle over her drooping shoulders. Her eyes were wide, but large bags sagged beneath them, and her clothes were dirty and creased. Despite her looks, she couldn't have been more than twenty-five.

'Sit down,' I said, drawing up a chair opposite my desk. 'My secretary told me you had a ghost problem.'

'It is difficult to know what to tell you,' she muttered apologetically. 'It's complicated.'

'Tell me everything,' I told her gently.

She opened her mouth and began to speak.

'I suppose it all started a long time ago,' she related hesitantly, a glazed expression on her face. 'I was born in Cardiff, where I lived until I was two. I had an older sister and a younger brother, but I was never really that close to them. My mother didn't work, but my father was in the army so we spent most of my childhood travelling from place to place to be near him when he was fighting. By the time I was eighteen, I had been to most places in Europe. My mother, however, decided that my sister Melanie and I needed a proper education, so we went to university in London. It was while I was there –' She paused. 'It was while I was there that my parents and brother were killed in a fire.'

She stopped speaking, her eyes swimming with tears. It was a while before she could continue, and I could think of nothing to say to fill the empty silence.

'In her will my mother left me a large old house on the Yorkshire moors that had been derelict for nearly twenty years. When I finished university last year, I moved in and began to fix it up. A short while later, I began to be awoken by loud noises in the night, and would find whole rooms upturned. The first few times I thought I was being burgled, although nothing was ever taken. But more recently, things have begun to be damaged and destroyed, and strange messages in white chalk have appeared on the walls. Two weeks ago I awoke to the sound of running water, and found the downstairs of the house was flooded. I came to wonder if I was being haunted. These last few days, I've enquired at several organisations relating to psychic studies, and one of them suggested that I come to you.'

I sat back in my chair, my head buzzing. I noticed that Katherine had fallen into a daydream, staring at the floor. A pile of papers fluttered to the ground, and Katherine blinked and sat upright, suddenly tense. I reached behind me to close the window that must have caused the breeze that disrupted the papers, only to find it was already shut.

'Miss Waters,' I asked, placing the mysterious breeze to the back of my thoughts, 'have any of these incidents ever happened during the day?'

'Yes,' she replied. 'Just a few days ago I fell asleep whilst reading a book and woke to find that a picture my father had painted had been slashed with a kitchen knife. I found the implement on the floor beside it.' She paused. 'Please say you'll come to the house and help me.'

I was intrigued by the case, and outlined our terms and conditions. She accepted them without question. I started my investigation at once, asking Katherine more about the messages on the walls. She showed me a photograph that she had taken of one message on a wall in the kitchen.

'All the messages say the same thing,' she informed me. The photograph showed an old tiled wall, with a hasty note scrawled messily across it.

The spirit lives in sleep.

After Katherine Waters had left, I talked to my colleague, James Lawrence, who started his working life as a psychiatrist and had moved into psychic work after a particularly disturbing incident involving one of his clients.

'As far as I can see, this is no ordinary haunting,' I told him. 'This ghost seems to act only when Katherine is either asleep or semi-conscious. '

'But what evidence do you have?' James asked.

'Well,' I told him, 'when she was in my office, she fell into a sort of trance and seemed oblivious to me and the rest of the world. As she sat there, a pile of papers fell off the desk, and yet when I turned around to shut the window I found it was already shut.'

'That doesn't prove anything,' James said grumpily. 'You're going to need more evidence than that.'

I surveyed him thoughtfully. 'I could always get evidence from her house.'

'Parker, you know as well as I do that "sleepovers" with single female clients, particularly those we've only just taken on, are out of the question. We lay ourselves open to all sorts of problems.' James was quite obviously not going to stand for any nonsense. Then he hesitated, seeing my expression. 'The only way you would be allowed to embark on a wild ghost chase would be if the victim was in immediate and serious danger.'

'And if she is?' I paused and waited with bated breath.

'If you really think that Miss Waters is in immediate danger, then I suppose you must go. A client's safety comes before anything else.' James didn't seem totally convinced, but I knew he'd come round.

'So far, the incidents don't appear to have been attacking her directly,' I informed him, 'but floods, vandalism and graffiti have been inflicted on Miss Waters' house, and dangerous objects have been found near her.'

'How long are you intending to stay?' James asked.

'Probably only a night or two,' I replied. 'Just enough to see what is really going on.'

'What about backup?' James enquired. (I'd known he'd bring it up at some point.)

'I'm going alone,' I told him hesitantly. 'And to put your mind at rest, I'll make sure that Katherine Waters is installed in an hotel for a couple of nights.'

'I'll give you a week away from the office to be on the safe side.' James began to clear away the files on his desk and I stood up to go.

'Noel,' James called after me and I turned around. 'Be careful.' I nodded, opened the office door and left.

I spoke to Katherine Waters on the telephone and arranged to spend two nights alone at Forest Lodge, investigating the mysterious ghost. Katherine said that she would spend a few days with her sister, while I did my preliminary work.

The same morning, I drove to Yorkshire and arrived at the house at about five p.m. It was quite obviously in need of repair. The windows were hanging off rotting frames, the once-stately iron gates were rusting, and the house itself was crumbling. The pillars supporting the front of the house looked ready to collapse.

I knocked on the front door a little too briskly and was appalled to see it fall inwards off its cracked hinges, which disintegrated in a cloud of grey dust on the cracked floor in front of me. Katherine emerged from a room on the left off a long and gloomy corridor.

'I'm sorry about your door,' I apologised.

'I shouldn't worry,' she muttered vaguely. 'Everything is falling to pieces in here.' She guided me through room after room of broken crockery, fallen shelves and wrecked furniture, describing what they should have been. The last room she showed me was her bedroom. Even here the ghost seemed to have been at work, breaking everything in sight. I flicked on a light switch, but nothing happened.

'The electricity wires were cut,' Katherine informed me simply. She handed me a packet of candles and a box of matches and walked across the room to stare out of the window. Following her, I saw that somebody – obviously her sister – was waiting outside in a dark blue Mini. Katherine picked up a travelling case from the bed, and left the room without turning round. I was left amidst the mayhem of the crumbling house, to watch her go.

After I had locked the house as best as I could for

the night, I took one of the candles from its box and climbed the rotten stairs to the loft. Even here the ghost seemed to have been busy, breaking up the floor and pulling down the beams. However, in one small corner, a narrow bookshelf seemed to have escaped the worst of the attack. One book in particular caught my eye. It was a small, leather-bound volume with faded gold letters etched into the cover. *Spirit*s.

I seemed to remember seeing this book in the office library, though I had never used it. Flicking through the stained pages, I found the section I was looking for. *Spirits of Sleep.*

However, to my surprise, the rest of the page had been savagely ripped away. I hurried back down-stairs, unzipped my briefcase, and turned on my mobile phone. I dialled James's number and waited anxiously, only to hear the mechanical operator informing me that the person I was calling was unavailable. I left a brief message asking for the book *Spirits* and impressing the importance it might have on Katherine's haunting. I hung up, slightly at a loss at what to do.

Then I noticed a pop-up message on my phone that I must have missed in my haste: *You have one new message*. I dialled my messaging system and heard James's familiar voice: 'Noel, it's James. Urgent news has recently come in. Katherine Waters was attacked at her sister's house with a pair of sewing scissors and has sustained serious chest injuries. She is stable in Weybridge Hospital, but I think you should come over here. Now.'

I was shocked at the news and realised the situation must be critical. I collected my belongings and rushed out to my car. As I drove, I realised that throughout the whole evening, I had not heard so much as a peek out of the ghost. Yet, Katherine Waters had been attacked. I still didn't know whether the attack had been ghost or human, but I intended to find out.

I arrived at Weybridge Hospital just as it was beginning to get light. James met me at the door and led me up to Katherine's room.

'What happened?' I asked anxiously, half-running along the corridor.

'That is for you to find out,' replied James severely. 'She was rushed to hospital after paramedics received a call from Katherine's sister, Melanie.'

'Was it a suicide attempt, or an attack?' I said, turning to face James.

'Attack.' James was blunt.

'Mortal or ghost?' I wasn't sure I even wanted to know the answer. James didn't reply. He simply pushed me briskly inside the door, pressing a small book into my hand. Katherine lay in a plain hospital bed, the crisp white sheets pulled up to her waist. Her chest was swathed in bandages, but as I entered she turned and gave me a weak smile.

'How are you?' I breathed.

'Could be better.' She sounded faint.

'Katherine,' I spoke gently but urgently, 'I need to know. Was this you, an intruder or a ghost?'

'I think it was a ghost,' she murmured. 'I was asleep, but woke as I felt pain. It was the weirdest thing. I could have sworn I saw my hand on the scissors. I couldn't have done it myself, could I, Noel?'

She was anxious now and I knew that despite what I thought, I had to reassure her.

'No,' I said quickly. 'You couldn't have done it.'

She looked at me. 'I've always feared wounds.'

'What else do you fear?' I asked her thoughtfully.

'Drowning, ghosts,' she gave a little laugh, 'and of course –' Katherine wasn't given the chance to finish as at that moment a nurse came hurrying in to the room and ordered me out.

'Visiting time is over,' she stated firmly. 'This patient needs rest.'

I started to protest, but she hustled me out of the room, closing the door behind us. I walked down the corridor to the cafeteria, aware of the nurse eyeing me suspiciously from her vigil by Katherine's door.

I found a corner table next to a window and got myself some coffee. The book James had given me outside Katherine's room was *Spirits*, the book I had asked him for. Flipping through the chapters, I found the one I was looking for and began to read.

Spirits of Sleep

These spirits are also known as Angslafgeists, which translates as 'ghosts of a feared sleep'. They take on the shape of a human being, controlling that human and inflicting pain and suffering on them until death. They only act when the human is asleep. They hurt by using their victim's fears, ending with the worst fear. The human appears to be sleepwalking and never knows exactly what happens, always waking up from their sleep in the same place. It appears the human is simply hurting themselves and the final attempt seems like suicide. These ghosts are rare but deadly.

I sat back in my chair, horror spreading through me. The ghost was part of Katherine, and was trying to kill her. That would explain why I had not even sensed a ghost at her house: it had left with her. I realised that if I didn't act fast, I would be unable to save her. Jumping up, I ran across the cafeteria, bumping into James Lawrence as I went.

'Noel!' He stopped me. 'Slow down. Where are you going?'

'James, I've got no time to explain,' I told him breathlessly. 'Katherine's life may be in very severe danger. I've found the ghost that's been haunting her.' I passed him the book.

'What's her greatest fear?' James asked suspiciously, scanning the page. 'It says that her fears will kill her.'

I thought hard. *Drowning, ghosts and . . . what?*

Fire!

'Fire, James, it's fire. Her parents and brother died in a fire. She told me her other fears are drowning and wounds. She's already been flooded and cut. This is her greatest fear, and it's going to kill her.'

James grabbed me by the arms. 'It only happens when she's asleep.'

'I was ushered out of the room to let her rest!' I cried exasperatedly. Half the cafeteria turned to stare and I dropped my voice, thinking fast. 'I reckon the only way to conquer the ghost is to make your greatest fear the ghost leaving. If I can make it to her room, I can make her fear the absence of the ghost and save herself.' I turned away from James, leaving him shocked and bemused, and bolted up the stairs.

I arrived outside the door to her room and paused, my hand on the handle. It felt warm. Pushing against the door, I fell inside, coughing amongst clouds of smoke and leaping flames. I flailed my arms madly and made for the burning hospital bed.

Then I realised. It wasn't the bed on fire, it was Katherine. Flames were licking at her arms and smouldering her legs and chest. Her hair had shrivelled up in the heat and her whole head was ablaze with red and orange flames. I knew there was nothing I could do to save her. The ghost had won.

Katherine's funeral was held a week later on a cold,

foggy day, and she was buried next to her parents and brother. Melanie and I were the last to leave the service.

'All my family have now been killed by fire,' she told me numbly as we walked down the path.

At the church gates, I turned and looked back across the cemetery. As I looked through the fog, I could have sworn I saw Katherine standing by her own grave. But was it her, or was it her tormenting ghost?

I resumed work the Monday after Katherine's funeral, still glum from the experience. Pete Feathercon greeted me with an enthusiasm I felt unable to return. Sensing my mood, Pete left me in peace all morning to finish reports. However, just before lunch he came into my office, carrying a blue folder.

'Mr Parker,' he ventured, 'I'm sorry, but what should I do with Miss Waters' file?'

I took the file from him and signalled he could leave. Opening it, I saw a photograph of Katherine pinned to the first page. In the background, I recognised Melanie. I smiled sadly, remembering her words at the funeral.

'All my family have now been killed by fire.'

Then it hit me.

'All my family have now been killed by fire.'

I realised this ghost's work was not finished. Neither was mine.

Fire House

Jenny Pritchard

Fire House

I knew that Mum and Dad had been house hunting for a couple of years now, but I didn't think they'd find one. I suppose, looking back, they did have a valid reason. Gramps was very old, and Mum wanted to be nearer to him. Gramps lived in a huge old house on his own, but it would make much more sense if he moved instead of us. I loved our house – it wasn't too big, and not too small either. Perfect in size. It was cosy, tall and narrow, a stylish Victorian terrace. It sat on the end of a long row of houses just like it. All my friends lived along my street, or at least near it. School was round the corner, I was happy.

Then Mum, after two years, finally found a house she loved. She didn't even consult my dad before putting an offer in. That was the kind of woman she was, business-minded and very pushy.

'Talk the hind legs off an elephant, she could, never mind a donkey,' my grandma always used to say. Mum was very attractive too, which she often used to her advantage. She had dyed blonde hair, which I had watched her mould and craft each morning for years. She had blue-rimmed eyes with long artificial sweeping lashes, and crimson lips. My dad, compared to most men, seemed rather weedy. Next to my strong-willed mother, he looked incredibly pathetic. So we had a brand new house to move into. And I hadn't even seen it yet.

'Are you ready, Fearne?' my mother shrilled, as I sadly looked up at our old house. It looked defeated, as if it had lost its battle to keep us.

It was an extremely warm July day, and the atmosphere was humid and sluggish. Dad was struggling to get three heavy cases into the Range Rover. His small legs looked almost bowed under the weight, and he was walking in a wobbly line. He dumped them into the boot, wiped his dripping forehead and walked round to the passenger side. He knew where he stood in the driving situation; my mother wouldn't even hear about Dad driving. She turned into a raving feminist when driving, and shouted about bad male drivers until she got where she was meant to be. I got into the back of the Range Rover. My legs stuck uncomfortably to the seat. My backpack was slumped on the floor where I had dumped it earlier. In it was a Game Boy and a couple of magazines. It would take hours to reach the new house.

Outside, my mother locked the front door and tucked the key snugly under the doormat, as arranged with the estate agent. She picked up two pet carry-cases from her feet, one in each hand. She held one up to her face.

'Hello babeeee! Aww, who's boootifuw? Mmm?' she cooed. She was talking to Norman, her prized

Persian cat. He was a grumpy creature with an ugly squished-up face – utterly adored by mum and loathed by most other people. In the carrier was my own cat, Bella. She was a fluffy black moggy with beautiful emerald eyes. Mum put one of the cases down, patted her hair, then picked it up again. She trotted down the front path in her pinstripe trouser suit and stilettos that she wore for her glamorous day job as a Marks and Spencer personal shopper. She put the cats on the seat next to me. Norman stared lazily at me with his big pale eyes. I swapped the cases so Bella was next to me instead. My mum stepped up elegantly into the car.

'Off we go!' she cried. She sounded delighted. My dad looked rather terrified at the prospect of leaving his beautiful terrace, which he had spent years renovating. A watery smile appeared on his face.

'Are you sure about this, dear?' he ventured.

'Of course I'm sure, Barry,' my mother snapped. She began to reverse out of the drive at high speed. A black Metro came flying along the avenue with its music blaring. Mum slammed on the brakes.

'Blooming imbecile!' she spat.

I could tell this was not going to be a pleasant journey.

After hours of stressful weaving through the city rush hour, we eventually came out on the other side of the chaos and reached the suburbs. Mum crawled along the streets in the Range Rover while my dad and I craned our necks to look at the huge houses lining the road.

'Number two-seven-eight Rise Avenue,' Mum kept repeating.

Eventually, we found it.

'Isn't it gorgeous!' my mother cried, her arms spread wide out. 'Just imagine what we can do with it, Barry!'

Dad swallowed. 'Isn't it a bit . . . well, big?' he asked nervously, pushing his glasses on to his nose again.

'Big is beautiful!' Mum said. 'Come on, then!'

We gathered what we could carry and set off up the huge front path. I picked up Bella's case and my backpack.

The house had looked big from the road, but up close it looked huge. The door had a small bronze gargoyle knocker and an elaborate keyhole.

'Where's the key?' I asked.

'Got it,' said Mum. She bent down to put it in the lock and twisted. It scraped and juddered until there was a click from inside, and the door creaked open.

We all stepped back as a cloud of dust puffed out of the doorway into the fresh air. My dad coughed and his eyes began to water. He was allergic to a lot of things, including dust.

'Oh Barry!' Mum said irately. She flicked a tissue from her sleeve in his direction, and he grasped it gratefully.

'In we go then!' she said with an excited grin. She stepped up the low mossy steps in to the hall. I followed. As I passed through the door I gave a gasp. It was beautiful – two huge curved staircases swooped around the outside of the room and met at the top. They took up most of the space. There was a strip of darker wood floor at each side of the stairway, as if there had once been a carpet going all the way up. The floor beneath my feet was black-and-white squares, visible even under the thick layer of dust.

'Oh!' my mother said in awe, with her hands clasped to her chest. She looked behind her for the light switch and found it. We looked up as light flooded the room from a decorative three-bulb fitting hanging from the domed ceiling. The ceiling was fantastic. It was white plaster carved into cherubs and other mythical beings. My mother gave a little squeal beside me. By now, Dad had joined us.

'Good grief!' he muttered.

I left them standing where they were and began to ascend one of the staircases. I stopped about halfway up. It was pitch black at the top. I lost my nerve and stopped playing brave.

'Mum! Dad? Come on, I want to explore!' I called.

'It's marvellous!' Mum said excitedly.

She turned to Dad, wrapped her arms around him and kissed him on the cheek.

'I knew you'd love it!' she whispered with a grin.

Dad didn't look too sure, but smiled anyway. She took his hand and pulled him up the stairs.

'It's a bit dark!' she commented when she reached me. She spun round to face Dad.

'Well! Go on, then! There's a light switch somewhere along there. The estate agent said the whole house was wired.' She folded her arms. Dad squinted his eyes into the darkness and swallowed.

'We haven't got all day, Barry dear,' Mum snapped.

He shuffled into the darkness. Soon there was a click, and the hall was filled with a dusky light.

There was a corridor with two doors along the wall. The first door revealed a huge bathroom, the second a study with floor-to-ceiling bookcases coated in dust and cobwebs, and a large oak desk. My mother kept giving little squeaks and gasps as she gazed around. The corridor ended in a narrow flight of stairs that doubled back on themselves to lead to the bedrooms. There were five bedrooms in all, with three of them facing the front lawn. There was also a loft, which mum quickly claimed for her painting studio.

I immediately knew what room I wanted as soon as we entered the third one. It wasn't as big as the first two, and the walls were covered with old-fashioned wallpaper, but I loved it. I felt drawn to it like a magnet. There was a high four-poster bed in the corner and a window seat. I could see the huge elm tree in the garden out of the window.

'This one's mine,' I announced.

'Are you sure? The other one's much bigger,' Dad said from the door.

'Darling! You must see the master bedroom, it's beautiful.' My mother's voice floated down the hall.

Dad left me alone to ponder the new house. I put Bella down in her carrier and lay on the bed. I glanced up at the ceiling. My jaw dropped.

It was covered in scorch marks and smoke stains. I stood up and spun slowly around, staring upwards. They covered the whole of the space, and were especially dark above the bed. I backed to the door frame.

'Mum!' I called, holding on to the door handle.

'What is it?'

'Look at this!'

I heard her open a door and get closer.

'What?' she asked, looking around, and following my gaze.

'Oh my God . . . Barry! Come here!'

Dad's reaction was pretty much the same as my mother's.

'Must have been quite an inferno,' he commented.

'It might be dangerous,' Mum said with a frown, pulling me back.

'No, the marks look like they've been there years,' Dad said. 'If it was going to fall in it would have happened a while back. We'll sand it down, then a quick coat of paint, and they'll disappear.'

Mum looked convinced. She let go of my shoulder.

'OK,' she said, 'if you're sure. I should complain to the estate agent. He never told me there'd been a fire.' She went back to the hall, muttering to herself.

'All right, love?' Dad asked, clamping my shoulder. It already hurt where Mum had held me back.

'Fine,' I said, wriggling free. When he left, I flopped on the bed again. I tried to decide what colour I would have for my new room. Blue, maybe, except blue was a cold colour. Maybe red or orange.

Later, my dad dropped the three suitcases and seven plastic shopping bags containing all my things on the floor, and I began to unpack. The removal van with all our furniture had arrived an hour ago and the men were moving everything in, directed by my mother.

My eye fell upon Bella, patiently waiting in her basket. I undid the catch and let her out. She rubbed around my legs with a small 'Meow!' but when I bent down to stroke her head, she froze. She was staring up at the blackened corner above my bed. Her fur stood on end, and her ears were pinned back to her head. She looked petrified.

'Bella?' I whispered. In a shot Bella was out of my room, and down the stairs. I followed her as quickly as I could. I stumbled on the second flight of stairs and reached the bottom just in time to see her streaking out of the front door as my mother came in with a plant in a gold pot. She watched as Bella whizzed past.

'Where's she off to?' she asked. 'Silly cat, she'll get lost. She should stay here like Norman, shouldn't she, Norm?' Norman was sat smugly on the bottom step of the opposite flight of stairs. Norman blinked. Mum smiled, and carried her plant into the new lounge. She popped it on the coffee table that she'd brought back from China.

'Perfect!' I heard her say to herself. She was having the time of her life, organising everything. The two removal men were trying to get Mum's leather sofa in through the door.

'No, no, no,' Mum said, clip-clopping out of the lounge with her hand held up. 'It'll never fit through there. Use the double door at the back.'

'Yes, ma'am,' one of the men mumbled, and they started to shuffled back down the steps.

After a hurried meal at nine o'clock, I went up to my room. I had may lamp plugged into an extension lead that led into the hall. There was only one ancient socket, in the hall, with various wires leading away into different rooms. The electrician had been booked to improve the lighting.

Sleepily, I put my book on the floor by my bed, and snuggled down in my sleeping bag. I clicked off the lamp, and settled down for a good night's kip. After a day driving with my mum, I definitely needed it!

I slept soundly until about three o'clock, when I

woke with a start. I looked at my glowing alarm clock on the upturned cardboard box I was using for a bedside table. I shut my eyes again, turned over, and sighed. Considering how tired I had been when I had dropped off, I didn't feel the slightest bit sleepy now. I opened my eyes again.

Before me was a blurred light. I sat up and rubbed my eyes. Suddenly my eyes focused, and I screamed.

I did not stop screaming for what seemed like a very long time, my eyes fixed on the figure before me. The sound of footsteps on the landing told me that my parents were coming to my rescue. I gave one long last cry, and passed out.

I came round to the sound of my mother calling. 'A wet towel Barry, not dry! Hurry up, you fool! Now give it to me. Honestly, Barry, I could have done it quicker myself.'

I felt her press it on to my forehead, and opened my eyes. Mum was peering over me. She had her eye-mask up on her head, and an extremely worried expression on her face. She looked much older without her make-up.

'Oh, she's come round. Sweetheart, what happened?' she asked, sitting me up. I was still on my bed, but the light was on and Dad was standing by the door.

I suddenly remembered. I must have made quite a face, because Mum paled and cried, 'Barry!'

'What happened? What?' she asked me, her eyes studying my face. She was biting her bottom lip.

'I . . . I . . .' I struggled to put what I had seen into words. 'A girl . . . she was there . . . smoke. Lots of smoke . . . and fire.'

Mum's face relaxed slightly. She gave a weak smile.

'A nightmare!' she said and hugged me. 'I thought you didn't have those any more?' I used to have terrible nightmares when I was about seven but I had slowly grown out of them. But I knew this was no nightmare.

'No. . .' I began to say.

Mum interrupted. 'Come on, back to sleep.' She tucked me in and got up to leave, and Dad switched off the light.

I stayed in the same position for a very long time. I didn't dare to move. I forced myself to keep my eyes open, even though I was afraid that the figure would come again. I was petrified that I would see what I had seen before. I knew that I never, ever wanted to see it . . . or her . . . again. I finally dropped back into a fitful sleep until morning, when I gratefully welcomed the light flooding through the window. My dressing gown was on the floor where I had thrown it last night, in my hurry to get to bed. I had a feeling I would not be hurrying for bed tonight.

The day passed slowly, and I enjoyed myself. I met two girls my age, who lived just on the next street.

We cycled around the avenues and they showed me a little of the neighbourhood. When I got back home I was surprised to see nearly everything in order. My mother was relaxing on her leather sofa, with a cocktail in her hand and her feet up. Dad was in the front garden, attempting to use a small trowel to dig out the monster weeds from the borders. He seemed to be producing a lot of sweat and not much border. He greeted me, and gladly took a break from kneeling down.

'Hi, Dad.' I told him about my new friends, and went in to spend the remainder of the evening watching television with Mum. Before I knew it, it was time for bed. The sun still had not set when I went upstairs. It had sunk in the sky and was hanging like a golden orb above the houses. I closed my new, deep red curtains. The sun still glowed through them, and made my room seem ablaze with scarlet and crimson. I shivered, despite the warmth, as I remembered last night's experience. Had it really been a dream? It had seemed so vivid, and I had passed out. Mum said I had been very hot; perhaps I had a twenty-four-hour fever? I shrugged to myself, changed into my pyjamas, and hopped into bed. After riding around the neighbourhood I was exhausted. I closed my eyes, feeling strangely calm as I dropped off to sleep.

At four o'clock I jerked awake in a surge of panic, as

I realised I had woken again in the middle of the night. A rust-coloured light flickered in front of me, reflecting in the mirror on the other side of the room.

She was there. A small girl stood at the foot of my bed, surrounded by an aura of light. My body tingled with danger and my senses screamed at me to move; get out. My nostrils picked up the stench of smoke, and my eyes saw licking flames. They curved up the walls, laughing and dancing as the little girl stared.

She was staring at me! I could feel my mouth morphed into an 'o' of fear. My eyes were wide and my limbs paralysed. The girl had been afraid last time, silently screaming, tears rolling down her face, engulfed by the flames. This time she stood there, while the flames licked at her.

A thought floated into my terrified mind. *This was her bed.*

Still she stared, straight ahead, unblinking. With a jolt, I realised that the flames were spreading. They were all around me, dancing, *burning* . . .

I thrashed my legs, my arms. Kept on twisting and writhing. Still she stared, flames reflecting in her eyes . . .

The husband and wife stood at the door, greeting the guests. The woman's eyes were red and puffy and a handkerchief was clasped in her fingers.

'I'm so sorry,' said a tearful lady as she shook the man's hand. 'She was such a lovely young lass.'

'I suppose you'll be selling the house,' one man said quietly.

'Yes, we're moving back to Weatherfield next week,' replied the blonde woman. Fresh tears slid down her cheeks.

The small group dressed in black gathered in the blustery churchyard. The vicar began his sermon, as the first shovel of earth was tossed into the grave on to the small black coffin that lay there.

Mr Brown crunched his cornflakes, as his wife cooked bacon by the stove. He was reading the newspaper.

'Pass your plate, Sam,' his wife said to their young son. She dealt out the bacon. It steamed on the plate as it lay next to a fried egg. ('Sunnyside up please, Mummy!')

Mr Brown turned to the properties page. His eye fell on the centre advertisement.

House for Sale

278 Rise Avenue, Westbrook.
A beautiful large Georgian house with historic features. Five bedrooms, lounge, kitchen, bathroom, study and attic. £250,000.

Mr Brown stopped crunching.

'Look at this, dear,' he said to his wife.

Mrs Brown switched off the gas and went to the table wiping her hands. 'That sounds nice,' she said. 'Good price.'

'Near your school, too, Sam.' Mr Brown looked over the paper at his son.

Later that day, Mr Brown wondered if he should ring the estate agent. It certainly seemed an excellent deal for such a big house. He decided he had nothing to lose. Ten minutes later he had arranged a visit to 278 Rise Avenue.

'I love it!' Mrs Brown said to her husband when the estate agent had left the room.

'We must buy it, darling! What do you think?'

'I must say, it is rather nice. Especially for such a low price!' he replied.

Their son's voice came from upstairs. 'Look, Mummy! Can this be my bedroom?'

Mr and Mrs Brown smiled. It seemed they had finally found the house they had been looking for. They followed their son's happy voice to the third bedroom. It was small with a window seat.

'Isn't it nice, Mum?' the little boy asked.

'Ooh, look at the ceiling!' said Mrs Brown.

'Nothing a lick of paint won't cover,' said Mr Brown.

They left the house ready to hand over their deposit to the estate agent. The sun hung low as the Browns went out through the bottom gate. Their son stood in the garden looking up at the house. He squinted against the sun with a frown. He thought he could see tendrils of smoke drifting in the third window. No. He must have imagined it.

'Sam!' his mum called.

From the window, two glowing figures looked out over the garden. Little Sam skipped out of the gate. The figures smiled, flames reflecting in their eyes.

Masterpiece

Liz Sutcliffe

Masterpiece

I'm not sure when it all started. I mean, I know I first noticed it the week of Ophelia's diagnosis, but it could have been going on for weeks, maybe months before. But the voices started around the time she stopped complaining about the headaches. We didn't believe for a second it was going away, or that the grim reaper might spare her the indignity of dying, or me a life of living with another relative. We knew that it wouldn't be long.

So I spent most nights lying awake in bed listening to the tapping sound of chisel against marble, and later to her slow, steady breathing through the thin wall that separated our bedrooms. It sounded so calm, so ordinary. You'd never have guessed that the owner of the blooming statue and the quiet breath also possessed a body that was eating itself from the inside out. I think that was what frightened me the most, really.

At first I put all the noises coming from Ophelia's studio down to my own imagination. I'd be sitting in the kitchen, biting my nails, or reading a book, and it would begin. Not as you might expect, with a drop in temperature: the reverse, in fact. A warm, dry wind would blow through the room, though the windows were closed against the biting autumn air, smelling like some sweet flower just beginning to decay. And I would look up, and hear it. Through the open door of the kitchen the whispering would start, a hundred voices giggling, and speaking words I couldn't make out. The first few times I thought there was somebody in there. I went charging into the cavernous studio, ready to spring to my aunt's aid and fight to the death against evil art-thieves. I never saw anybody, and I only once caught sight of a hazy fog floating just over a bemused-looking Ophelia's shoulder.

'What – what's that?' I asked. She was holding a delicate sculptor's brush in one hand and a cup of tea in the other. Her white-blond hair blew about her face in the mysterious breeze, and she was smiling at me in the same way she had for the last twelve years, ever since my parents' death had thrust me into her care. And I couldn't worry her, ill as she was.

'Sorry. Ignore me. I'm just confirming the belief I was given a lobotomy at birth.' I tried to smile.

'As if we needed confirmation,' she said with her usual laugh. She stepped aside and waved her arms dramatically at the half-formed statue that was emerging from the work of her long-fingered hands. 'What do you think?' she asked, knowing exactly what I would say.

That was the first time I saw it as anything more than a big lump of white rock, and I gasped. Anyone would have. My aunt was a great artist, anyone will tell you that. Her paintings and sculptures sell for small fortunes, most of which are waiting for me in a trust. But this was incredible. The beginnings of a winged human blurred suddenly, and before I knew what was happening I was sitting on the floorboards with my head in my hands.

She knelt down beside me, and I felt her hands on my shoulders. 'It's not that bad, is it?' A laugh bobbed up like a helium balloon through my pathetic sobs. I shook my head vigorously, and gulped in a few desperate breaths of air as I took in her face – the face of the person who made me what I am – and cried even harder. I flung my arms around her shoulders, and only succeeded in pulling her on top of me, and making us crash in a heap of legs and arms into an easel.

I stayed there, wrapped in her comforting arms, for a while. She just stroked my hair. Eventually, of course, we had to get on with life. I went back to reading, and wandering in the garden, never daring to stray further than the corner shop.

Every scrap of medical evidence said that at any moment Ophelia might keel over and die, with no warning at all. And after a couple of weeks, I began to believe this might happen. The headaches came roaring back, accompanied by voices that were almost shouts. Every time I came bursting into her room, desperately looking for some sign the hounds of hell weren't coming, she was standing by her precious statue, one eyebrow disappearing under her soft blond fringe. I was terribly afraid, but we had a kind of peace.

It didn't last.

'Did you know,' she said one morning, scrutinising the glorious white figure, 'that there's a tribe of American Indians who believe that if you create one perfect thing, your life purpose is achieved and you'll die? You have no reason for living after that.'

I'd been placing yet another cup of coffee on her table. My hand jerked, and coffee slopped over the side on to the scratched surface.

'No, I didn't know that.' I tried to sound normal, but I could hear how my voice squeaked. It wasn't the implied belief that what she was creating was perfect, or the idea she might die as soon as her statue was finished. What terrified me was the idea that I was not a reason for her to keep living.

I knew my aunt was conceited. She had reason to be. Sometimes her air of superiority made me want to slap her, but mostly I put up with pompous announcements like, 'I will save Art,' and 'I've always known I'm going to be special.' But I'd had the idea in my head that it was really *me* she lived for; me, not the art critics she tried to please. I tried to ignore the way my throat closed up, and my vision blurred with tears of hurt. A brief silence passed. I breathed in the vaguely rancid air and listened to

Ophelia humming. Suddenly it just burst out of me.

'What about me?' I demanded. 'Don't I make your life worth living? Aren't I worth more than a lump of rock?' I clapped my hands to my mouth, trying to force the hateful words back into my heart. An injured look, mirroring my own, flashed across Ophelia's face.

'No!' she gasped. 'No! How can you say that?' I could see her trying to turn the hurt into anger. 'It's not like that at all!' She threw down her chisel and it clattered across the floorboards, making a dint in one.

'God, I just want it to be perfect! I want the world to know I existed! I want to have been real! Oh, God, I don't want to die.' As we had a few days before, she slumped to the floor. 'Oh, God, I don't want to die.'

For a moment I stood stock still, vindictively pleased to see her upset, moved to any emotion other than smug pleasure for a change. But then all the things she had done for me flooded in, and I skidded across the floor to her and wrapped my arms around her, awkwardly at first, and then in the same way I had for the last fourteen years. My guilt flowed in tears.

'It will be perfect, it will,' I promised wildly. And then, it seemed as though more than one person was crying. The warm breeze drifted in, and the hair stood up on the back of my neck. I stared at my aunt in shock, feeling my heart pick up. It was as though a faint mist was rising from her skin, coiling around her body like a delicate robe.

'What's happening?' I asked, beginning to panic. 'Auntie, what's happening?' I raised my hands to my mouth, looking in fear at the way the fog twined around her body. Abruptly, she stood up.

'I have to finish it, it's almost too late,' she said, her eyes blank and unfocused. 'It's my only way out . . .'

'What are you saying?' Fright leaped into my voice. She grasped my hands, and I recoiled. It was like being grabbed by a snowman. 'You have to help me!' she almost screamed. 'You have to, it's my only chance! Please, help me!' She grabbed at me again, and this time I couldn't shake her off. She clung like a vice, and I clung back. I watched in a kind of fascinated horror as the fog twisted its way up my own arms, sinking into my skin. It felt as though water was trickling through my skin, into my bloodstream and freezing its way to my heart. Compared to the warmth of the ominous wind, it felt terrible, as though I was dying.

I don't know how long we spent like this; my small, clumsy hands enveloped in her delicate ones. The ice within her poured into me, and it was painful and awful. But as it happened, it was as though some deep and sacred knowledge was transferred as well. If Ophelia could finish her statue, make it perfect and beautiful, she would be released before the cancer took her. And I could help.

Eventually, she let go. I reeled backwards and fell against the table, upsetting the mug of coffee. The brown liquid spread across the floor, and it seemed beautiful in comparison to the icy terror of whatever Ophelia had done to me. I scooped up the cup and poured whatever was left of the lukewarm coffee down my throat with one swallow. The warmth spreading out through my body was wonderful.

I looked up at my aunt. Her statue stood by her with its wings raised above its head, as though mocking the way Ophelia stood so limply. She looked up at me shrewdly, and for a moment I thought she might apologise. But all she said was, 'Help me.'

A huge part of me wanted to run away, screaming. Another part wanted to go to bed and sleep for a thousand years. But I walked over and picked up a sweeping brush and began to clean up the area around her feet as she worked at her statue. Though her body moved jerkily and ungraciously, her hands moved with an elegance I had never seen before. There were miles to go; all it was so far was a head, half a torso and a pair of wings. The rest disappeared into a block of white marble. But we worked for hours.

She was getting weaker and weaker every hour, as though all her health was slowly pouring into it. Each minute a new, perfect detail emerged, a finger, an eyelid, and a hint of feathers on the outstretched wings. We worked in silence; the only sounds were her increasingly ragged breathing, and the sound of the steel against the stone. I felt as though I was in some kind of trance. She never said a word, she simply had to look at me and I would sweep, or dust a pocket of powder away, or hand her a piece of sandpaper.

I didn't get tired, or bored. As night came, I first understood where the idea of it gathering comes from – the shadows enlarged and clumped together, making what might have been an angelic figure into a force of darkness. That figure became increasingly perfect as it got harder and harder to see. Without thinking about it too much I flicked on the table lamp, and the shadows contorted and vanished. Again the mist floated on our skin, and again I felt chilled to my core. Random thoughts chased their way across the surface of my brain, all saying, 'This is stupid,' or, 'What are you doing?' But we battled on, and I don't think I could have stopped, even if I had wanted to. I didn't.

All my life I had longed for this, the chance to be useful, the chance to do more than make cups of coffee. At around midnight Ophelia offered the handle of her favourite chisel, and I wanted to cry again. I took it in my hand and, instinctively knowing what to do, carved off some of the useless chips hiding the place the line of the calf should be. It was as though this beautiful figure was hiding just under the surface of the white stone, waiting for us to reveal it in its shining glory. I raised the chisel to strike again, my heart skipping with wild joy.

But as I began to bring it down, to hack away at the stone that dared to cover up the angel within, my heart stopped beating. I reeled, dropping the tool. Clutching at my chest, I staggered away from Ophelia. She never even looked at me; just continued to tease out the shape of the other leg. Without warning, and to my great relief, the roar of blood started up again in my head, and my heart began to thud. With the blood, warmth spread back to my body. I held up my hand to my face and stared at the purplish-blue fingers. The soundtrack of sinister whispering quietened slightly. For a moment, the doubting part of me surged up and nearly won. I almost ran. But then the feet came.

The statue was supposed to be perfect. I don't know what 'perfect' is, whether it's simply the absence of flaws, or something deeper and more mysterious. But it was the only word I could think of as the left foot of our angel began to emerge. It looked poised and ready to kick off from the ground, as though the whole heavy thing was about to launch out the window into the dark night beyond. And, more than that, the feet were Ophelia's. With my regained clarity of thought, I stared at the thing's face. It didn't look like her. While Ophelia's face was narrow and feminine, this creature had an oval, androgynous one, with a perfectly straight nose compared to the once-broken one Ophelia had. But there was something of my aunt in what we had created.

My resolve strengthened. I was going to set her free. I went around with the brush again.

The darkest time of night is right before dawn. It certainly seemed so then. The shadows made us an island in the dark, carving and chipping away at this person. It got easier to think of this statue in that way as we worked. As the hours passed, I confused in my mind, more and more, which was my aunt and which was an inanimate piece of stone. Whether this was just lack of sleep and food, I don't know. But it seemed to me that the white haze around Ophelia was slowly but steadily flowing towards the statue. She seemed to get thinner and paler before my eyes. As we began to work at the finer details, she swayed on her feet and coughed worryingly.

We finished just before dawn. With the slightest brush at the hair with a thin piece of wire, Ophelia stepped back from her creation and simply stood. I waited, a small brush hanging loosely from my hand. I didn't know what to do or expect. Just as I was beginning to shout at myself for getting carried away, it happened.

The white smoke around Ophelia's body disappeared. She gasped, sucking air into her tired lungs. I started towards her, but before I could reach her, she crumpled to the floor. I gave a little gasping scream, but still couldn't move towards her. She inhaled deeply, unable to lift her head up from its bed of stone chips. As I stood, paralysed, one of her hands crept out to the creature. It crawled up the base, and when it reached the leg, grasped tightly.

For a moment I thought the fog had returned. But it wasn't ethereal cloud that gathered around Ophelia's body, it was light. It glowed out of her white skin, brightest where skin touched stone. Then, without warning, it flashed so bright I instinctively screwed up my eyes. When the after-images faded, my aunt had disappeared.

I thought my heart was going to explode with joy and sorrow, mingling together in it like a cocktail. But before I could take in the vanishing of a full-grown woman, something even more incredible happened.

The statue moved. Not quite as a human would move. For the first time I really screamed. The head of that terrible white thing swivelled to face me, and its lips curled into a familiar smile. With wild sobs pouring from my mouth, I watched as the statue stretched out its glorious wings and, as I had imagined an hour before, took off.

Two metres of marble rose into the air like a bird, wings flapping with a controlled grace. It crashed through the window with the worst sound I've ever heard in my life, before stretching out into the early morning like a hunting owl. I broke the paralysis and ran to the hole, staring out after the escaping statue. I looked into the room, seeing her body really was gone. As the sunlight streamed into the room, I crouched beneath the window. I wept in grief and triumph.

I live with Aunt Evelyn now. She isn't Ophelia, but I am happy, mostly from knowing that Ophelia didn't truly die. I don't know if it was her spirit that made the statue fly, and I've never seen it again. But each night, like her, I dream of stretching wings to the sky and flying away.

Waking Asleep

Jonathan Tidmarsh

Waking Asleep

The tramp was dead and it was entirely my fault.

The post-mortem revealed that he had not drowned but died of unknown causes. Strange, it seems, for a man to be found face down in a river but not to have actually drowned. It occurred to me it was even stranger that not even two hours after parting from his company, he was dead. When I read about his death it appeared that it was simply a coincidence, but this disturbed me the most: the night before I met him, I dreamed his death.

Nobody believed me. I don't think anybody ever will. To start with, I didn't even believe myself. I thought I had killed him, but I wasn't sure.

Which is why, one week later, I had to go back.

'They found him right over there.' The woman said, pointing her huge forearm protruding from a large T-shirt that billowed in the wind.

He already knew how, where and when they had found him. The tramp had been face down in the river, caught on a trolley that had been thrown over the bridge. He even knew which supermarket the trolley was from: Iceland.

She stopped pointing and let her arm fall to her side. 'Poor fellow, probably couldn't take it any more,' she said. 'The years of being alone on the streets – I wouldn't be able to handle it, and of course he was in a terrible state . . .' She paused for a moment, thinking about what to say next, but she said nothing. They just stood there silently gazing across the water. As they did, he caught a glimpse of her wondering what his interest was in this man's death. Her hair was thick and black and wavered in the slight breeze, which the wind had now become. He wondered if she had a family; children and a husband. It was possible she had all of these, and just as possible that she had none.

'You don't say much, do you?' she stated with a warm smile spreading across her face. At that moment he realised how silent he had been, and how disconcerting it must have felt for her.

'I was just thinking . . .' he started hesitantly as he thought of something to continue the sentence. She smiled again, and in the embarrassment he forgot about finishing.

'Thinking about what?' she asked.

If this is going to work, he thought to himself, *I will have to get to know her; I will have to do it exactly how it happened last time*. He began to say something but stopped almost as the words hit his lips.

What if she did have a family? What if she did have children and a husband?

If this really is happening, and if it does happen again, I'm going to deprive them of her forever. Do I really want to do that? His conscience had kicked in and he realised what it might mean. But he also realised that if it was indeed happening, then she was already dead.

'I'm sorry.'

She was puzzled by this statement but said nothing about it, which pleased him. It meant he wouldn't have to try to explain himself, at least not now anyway.

She had three children, two girls and a little boy. Her husband was on a tour of duty in the Middle East. She did have a family.

He was about to tear it apart.

That night, he couldn't sleep: he didn't want to sleep. He knew that if he closed his eyes for a second he would see it. Her death. Her passing away. And it would be all because of him. At that moment he was still in a kind of severe shock. He couldn't quite believe what was happening. Was it true that he could dream of someone's death and that the dream would become reality? Had that tramp's departure simply been coincidence? Or was it really the truth? He drifted restlessly to sleep. The dream was harsh and vivid. The woman being hit by a car, pinned against a wall, and dead in a matter of seconds.

'Excuse me, hi, I'm looking for one of your employees. She's called Anne Turner – has she come into work yet?'

The receptionist looked robotically at him. 'I'll just check for you.'

'Thanks.'

She gave him a look that suggested she did this quite often, and was sick of doing it. Something flashed up on the computer monitor.

'No, she hasn't arrived yet.'

Panic swept over him like a cold wind. It had happened. The receptionist looked up for a moment, and then checked some papers.

'She's due in any moment now.' She looked up again. 'There she is!' She directed with her arm.

He smiled with relief. This meant it was just a coincidence, that the nightmare was a horrible coincidence. He was free. Yet at that moment he had a flashback of the horrible occurrence. A red car swerved round the corner as she stepped on to the pavement.

It wasn't a flashback. The incident had not happened yet. It was happening now.

His mother was at home watching the news when he got in. She sat silently eating a sandwich; a cup of tea was on the small table to her right. Her slender body was motionless in the seat, her mind pensively dormant. The light from the late afternoon lit up her face in such a way that her eyes glistened. She appeared to have been crying, but he rarely noticed when she wasn't.

'Do you want something to eat?' she asked.

He didn't know. All he could think of was the woman's face as she died, stricken with fear and pain. What made the whole experience worse was that, as he had run past the accident, the car appeared to be empty.

'I can make you some sandwiches or you can do something yourself.'

He turned to face his mother, weighing up whether to tell her or not. She looked at him and her expression changed to one of concern. She knew something was wrong. Then he collapsed on to the floor with tears streaming down his face.

He told her everything, sometimes repeating himself in his confusion. He kept saying how utterly useless he felt, how unfair the whole situation was, how unfair the world was. And it wasn't fair, he had no control over any of it and that was what scared him the most. He doubted that he could even warn people of what was going to happen. And even if he did, he doubted if they would take any notice. The world was too large and moving too quickly for people to take any notice of premonitions of death.

His mother's expression and the sound of her reassuring 'hmmms' meant he didn't even know if she believed him. This disheartened him even more, because it told him that he had absolutely nowhere to turn. They sat together, silently now, in the approaching darkness. The room felt suddenly very large and intimidating to him. He wondered what was going to happen. He was almost certain that she was going to die next. He did not know how, but he knew he would see it the next time he closed his eyes. Then his world would be torn apart, like the lives of those children whose mother he had taken away. In the darkness he thought how cruel the world was. He had taken their mother; he would next take his own.

How long would this go on? Until he was the last surviving human being?

Until they realised who was doing it and then kill him? Or until he killed himself? He had to sleep some time, and each time someone he knew would die.

He wondered why his mother had not died earlier; he wondered why it was the tramp, and why it had been Anne Turner. Then he fell asleep.

. . . the hand drew the blade over the left wrist. It stung as the thin-edged metal pierced the skin and released a crimson tide. Convulsing gushes rippled over the folds of the hand that grew pale and limp. The hand attempted a second slash but the knife had already fallen into the sodden, red carpet stain . . .

He woke to an empty house. She was gone. That was how it would all end for her, he thought to himself, and I have seen it happen before she knows. To him it seemed only fitting; it even made sense. His mum had been depressed since Dad had died ten years back. Maybe she even wanted to die. Maybe it was her right to see him again. To be reunited with the one whom she loved so much. She had never thought about remarrying, it just hadn't occurred to her that that was possible. 'You can only, truly love one person in your lifetime,' she always used to say. He didn't know if that was true. But it seemed to make sense now that she was gone.

He hadn't really known his father, who had died after a car crash. The truck driver had fallen asleep at the wheel. The road was busy. It was raining. It was dark. He remembered playing with a toy car while Mum and Dad spoke softly to each other. Then he wanted to say goodbye. Back then he didn't understand where his dad was going. But then, would any four-year-old?

There was virtually no food in the house. A half-empty bottle of milk stood alone on the topmost shelf of the fridge. Below it, a crust lay encased in its plastic wrapper. Tuesday was usually Mum's shopping day, but he guessed she would not be doing any of that today. He didn't know where she was. Could be down by the stream, or the abandoned farm. Anywhere to be alone, he thought, for space and solitude. Somewhere that when she was found, it would all be too late.

The café was small and out of town. Its

atmosphere was quiet and reassuring. He had consciously decided on this, fearing any more deaths. It wasn't totally empty, there were a few people sitting and sipping coffee whilst reading the paper or daydreaming. None of the people knew or recognised him. That was the way he liked it, for now anyway, he was nobody. He thought he had given up the right to be someone when he started killing people. He drained his coffee mug, leaving a tiny amount of residue in the bottom, then sat back in the plastic-moulded chair and looked out into the afternoon. *Who else out there would die because of me?* he wondered.

Who will I dream of next, and how will they die?

He genuinely believed he had nowhere to go, nobody to turn to and no real point to existence. He had an incredible gut feeling that there was no point to anything, and nothing he could do. This was it. This was rock bottom. He felt as though the entire world was against him, that no matter what he did, he would fail. He could not stay awake for ever. It was inevitable that someone else was going to die. There was only one thing he could do to stop it.

The café had emptied, and all of a sudden he felt very peaceful. He felt at ease with himself. In that moment he seemed to forget his worries and was able to relax, just for a little bit. He put everything out of his mind, looked out into the townscape dappled in evening sunset light, and the shrouded shadows where the light had already faded. He thought about his situation for a second, and with the shining rays of evening light there seemed to be a small crack of hope in the impenetrable wall of despair. He smiled to himself.

'That's the first smile all afternoon,' exclaimed a voice from behind the counter. 'We're closing up now, sorry.'

Startled, troubles back, he turned to face the person. A girl about his age, shorter than he was, with red hair that outlined her face and flared out just above the shoulders. She was leaning on the counter and smiling at him. The name badge said Molly. Caught off guard, he replied, then realising what that could lead to, he cursed himself, and rushed out of the café with the girl calling after him. He didn't turn back to find out why.

Either way he knew who was going to die next.

Everything was silent. This was the end. The knife in his right hand, quivering as his heart pumped harder, more frequently, forcing blood around his body one last time as he pulled all the will he had left to put an end to his suffering, and to save the lives of many who would come after him. He slashed once and hesitated, momentarily hypnotised by the crimson tides emerging from his wrist. A small pool of blood emerged by his side. A red stream running over his arm, through the folds in his limp hand and through the gaps between his fingers, eventually meeting in the same sodden red stain. He tried to slash once more, but the knife had already fallen from his grasp.

Her shoes crunched the gravel as she came to a halt just outside the house. She looked at the address she had found in the wallet. It matched. A street lamp flickered into life and buzzed momentarily. Another followed a few seconds afterwards, as if taking a cue. Brushing the creases out of her shirt she stepped up, and rang the doorbell.

No answer.

In a confusion of anger and disappointment she dropped the wallet through the letterbox, and turned away to walk home, only to be apprehended in the headlights of a car pulling up on the drive. She considered just walking on but while she hesitated, the car door opened.

'Hello, are you here for Martin? Is he not in?'

She felt nervous at meeting someone else that knew him, probably his mother.

'Yeah, he left his wallet at the café – just dropped it off for him.'

'How very kind of you. Give me a hand with the shopping and you can wait for him inside – he could use a friend right now.'

The girl began to say that she didn't really know him and was just here to drop off his wallet, but the woman started talking about how depressed he was.

It seemed right to pick up two bags and follow her into the house. Once over the threshold the world became warmer, but darker at the same time. This was a home, but had not housed a family for years. The hall had piles of unopened post on the sideboard. There was a picture hook, but no picture. The kitchen had two chairs, side by side, only one with shoes beneath it. Pale rays reached in from the windows, trying to bless the room with light but it seemed feeble, almost not trying. A fluorescent tube clicked into bright but inoffensive light.

The boy's mother left the room momentarily to call up the stairs to Martin. They both waited. No voice, no movement, nothing.

'I'll go up and get him, you can go through into the sitting room if you like.'

Molly disappeared from view but she could be heard climbing the steps quietly.

She went into the room, not really knowing why she was there, and sat down on a couch. A letter shivered on the table, rose and fell invitingly within her reach. She curiously picked it up, and read.

To the person who reads this –
I have gone away where I can sleep for ever and not hurt any other people. I was killing people every time I slept. I would dream of their death and then the next day they would be dead, all because of me. I killed them all – the tramp, Anne Turner and my

own mother. I didn't want to wake up and find someone else was going to be dead. I didn't want her to be dead. She didn't deserve to die.
I'm sorry for everything.
Martin

At his funeral, Martin's mother placed a note with the wreath of flowers. It read:

The trolley was from Tesco.
The car was blue.
The third death was your own.

A Division of Myself

Rebecca Wait

A Division of Myself

Julian is bored. He is bored of Tom and Simon, he is bored of playing snooker in the dim, smoky pub and he is bored of the pretty, empty-headed girl hanging on his arm. He is possessed by a feeling of unreality.

'Your shot.'

'What?' Tom is speaking to him.

'Your turn. It's your turn.'

Wearily, Julian takes up his cue and aims at the white ball. He hits it with more force than he intends and it skids dizzily across the green felt, bounces off the side and comes to a rest near its original place. Julian watches it dispassionately. How he hates this game. He only started playing it because Michael and the others had gone through a snooker phase a while back, and now Tom and Simon seemed to want to play it as some sort of tribute to Michael.

Michael would find this extremely amusing, Julian thinks sourly.

Tom is crowing in delight over Julian's missed shot (You're pathetic, Julian tells him silently) but Simon just laughs and says, 'You should stick to knitting, J.' Julian thinks how kind Simon always is, and how rarely anyone notices. What's more, Simon actually believes everyone else is as guileless as he is. Simon is an idiot.

He shakes Sandra off his arm and walks over to the bar to get himself a drink. He doesn't extend the offer to the others. He's bored of them.

To a casual observer, Julian is unremarkable-looking. His expression is blank, a mask of concealment, and he twirls the snooker cue idly between his fingers. But his face is strangely pale in the gloom and his eyes have a distant look, which, upon looking closer, might pass for dazed. Sandra, infatuated and slightly desperate by now, doesn't notice this. She dreamily interprets the detachment in his eyes as part of his 'deep sensitivity'. She resolves to try again. As Julian is finishing his drink, she flits over and hops on to the stool beside him. She says, 'Not your favourite game?'

'What?'

'Snooker.'

'No,' Julian says. 'Too much hanging around. It was always much more Mike's thing, wasn't it?'

'Yes.' She is awkward. 'Do you miss him?' she adds, rather desperately, because she can't think of anything else to say. She is embarrassed, flustered. Julian observes this in silence and is faintly amused.

Unnerved, she continues, 'Because, you know, twins are like, really close, and you and Mike, well, um – you know.' She tails off. Julian feels a savage pleasure in witnessing her discomfort. Stupid girl.

'I kind of feel like he's still with me,' Julian explains. She looks moved. Julian turns away to hide his grin.

Michael would have enjoyed that.

A Division of Myself

* * *

When Julian gets home he goes straight to the piano, and lifts the heavy walnut lid. He seats himself and touches the white keys, cold and patient beneath his fingers. He begins to play. It's something old, Beethoven, he can't remember which, and he can't remember the ending. He rummages around in the chest by the piano and draws out the sheet music. He starts to play again. It's beautiful. He forgets. For the time being, there is only the music.

' "If music be the food of love, play on . . ." ' a voice declaims dramatically behind him. Julian starts and turns round. Someone is leaning against the doorpost watching him; a boy of his own age with the same dark hair and sharp features. An exact copy, a perfect division of himself. Except – no. Closer, there is something wrong with the mirror image; there is something in its expression that is warmer than Julian's (perhaps it is the eyes) and it is wearing a lopsided grin that is never seen on Julian's face, though it is as familiar to Julian as the lines on his own palms.

'Piss off, Michael,' says Julian.

'You're charming tonight,' his twin comments, sidling further into the room and seating himself on the coffee table behind the piano. 'Lucky Sandra.'

'I'm trying to *play*.'

'So I see. Keep trying and you might manage it one day.'

Julian glowers at Michael and strikes up again

loudly, assaulting the keys viciously and pressing his foot on the pedal. Their cat, Will (Shakespeare), curled up in the corner, flinches elegantly and narrows his slanting eyes at Julian.

'How is the lovely Sandra?' shouts Michael above the resounding notes.

'Annoying. Like you.'

'Right. You don't deserve her. She should be with someone like me.'

'You're welcome to her.'

'I think it might be slightly hard to arrange.'

Julian stops playing. 'If it bothers you, I won't go out with her again. I don't care either way.'

'Screw that,' replies Michael cheerfully. 'That's totally pointless. Go out with her.'

'I don't even like her.'

'That's because you're a prat. So see her for my sake – "under love's heavy burden do I sink",' Michael quotes emphatically.

'Oh, go away. Go and visit Shakespeare, since you're such mates. He's out there somewhere, right?'

'Shakespeare isn't dead. Shakespeare liveth on . . .'

'Bugger off.'

Michael leaves, whistling. 'You could do a lot worse than Sandra!' he calls from the next room. Julian returns to his music.

Michael is still there the next morning. Julian wanders downstairs to find his brother sitting cross-

124

legged on the floor of the sitting room with his playing cards spread about him. Michael is crazy about card games. Julian watches him deftly flip the cards over in turn, muttering to himself. Julian plays along with the game in his mind for a moment, but Michael's thin white hands move so swiftly, Julian soon gets lost.

'You should get out more,' Julian advises him. 'Too many card games aren't healthy.'

'Since when have you been life and soul of the party?'

Julian seats himself by Michael. 'Well, at least I haven't devoted my life to the sacred pursuit of solitaire.'

'Least I can play snooker.'

'Least I'm not obsessed with Shakespeare.'

'I'm not obsessed. And at least I don't play the piano with my eyes closed.'

'Neither do I!' retorts Julian indignantly.

'Don't you? You should try watching yourself when you play. It's very funny.'

'Want a game of Cheat?'

So they play, Michael winning every game with ease and laughing at Julian's ineptitude. Halfway through their third game comes the sound of the front door slamming. They look at each other, and Michael lays down his cards.

Minutes later, a plump, wan-looking woman with too many wrinkles on her forehead enters the room, carrying shopping bags. She doesn't see Michael. She sees only Julian; Julian sitting on the floor by himself with what seems to be *two* hands of cards dealt out in front of him. Something tugs painfully inside her. It is a familiar feeling. With well-practised firmness, she discounts the unease. She's just being neurotic. Julian's a survivor. Always has been. She manages to keep her voice normal as she enquires, 'Who are you playing cards with, darling?'

'Myself. You know. Solitaire.' His face is blank. Is it normal? Should he be this unreadable?

She says, 'You know, Julian, if you, um, ever want to play cards with me, just ask. Any time, right? I like cards.'

'OK. Thanks.' She leaves the room.

Michael mutters, 'I worry about Mum.'

'She'll be OK,' Julian says. 'I was always her favourite.'

'Yes,' Michael agrees, 'I expect she particularly liked the time you nearly got expelled from school for attacking Mrs Sullivan with a paintball gun.'

'You know perfectly well I was aiming for Tom.'

For a while they bicker companionably over their cards. Suddenly, Michael leans forward and says, 'Ready to hear something sappy?'

'Whenever you open your mouth.'

'I once had this dream,' Michael confides. 'It was really strange. There was this old guy, in a kind of ragged cloak with a long white beard. Really filthy –

looked like a tramp or something. But he sort of – well – *shone.'*

'*Shone?'*

'Yes. Anyway, he was speaking in this strange language, but I understood him. And he told me that whenever a soul entered heaven, white feathers fell to Earth from nowhere.'

Julian raises his eyebrows. 'That's sweet, dear. White feathers?'

'Yeah.'

He stares straight at Julian and there's a moment's stillness in which the brothers stare at each other, neither willing to speak. Julian remembers years ago when Will the cat had caught a pigeon and left it broken and dying on their patio, still cooing feebly. 'Leave it, boys,' their father had said. 'It'll be dead by the end of the day.' But Michael had wept over the bird's pathetic end, and refused to leave it, forcing Julian to sit with him on the warm concrete for a whole afternoon, wincing at the bird's pain-wracked cries, until Julian decided enough was enough and stamped on the pigeon's head.

He'd just been putting it out of its misery, he'd tried to explain to Michael later, but Michael had sobbed and refused to listen. But they were young and Michael had forgotten soon enough, much sooner than Julian, who never forgot how the dirty, blood-stained white feathers had remained stuck to the ground for weeks after the rest of the bird had been buried. And the nightmares he'd had. Now, he shudders and looks away from his brother.

Then the spell is broken; Michael begins to chuckle, and then to laugh loudly. 'Dear me! White feathers? A visit from God in my dreams? You really are gullible these days. It's quite sweet, really. Must be the absence of my shrewd influence.'

Julian glares at him.

Michael is laughing his laugh, the one only he does, the low chuckles interspersed with high-pitched giggles; Michael's ill-matched laugh. Julian smiles now, in spite of himself.

Michael continues, unwilling to relinquish the joke just yet, 'The look on your face! Anyone'd think you'd seen a ghost . . .'

'That isn't funny.'

When Julian drifts blearily downstairs for school the next morning, Michael has gone. Julian never wonders where Michael goes on these occasions. As if by private agreement, it is never mentioned between them. But Michael always reappears, and then they continue as before.

And indeed, some days later, Julian trudges upstairs after school to find his bedroom door ajar. Vaguely unnerved, for reasons he cannot quite grasp, he pauses and calls, 'Mike? Mike, are you . . .' The words die in his mouth as his eye falls on a sight that freezes his heart. Swaying slightly where he stands, he grips the banister: just visible behind the foot of the door, lie several grubby white feathers. He forces himself to comprehend. *White feathers.* A soul enters heaven. The words circle round his brain like a distorted mantra. He tries to shake them clear, dizzying himself. The monstrous little feathers swim before his eyes. He sits down weakly at the top of the stairs, reeling.

It is like this, several hours later, that Michael finds him.

'What's up with you?'

Julian has not noticed his brother approach, and is ill-prepared to disguise the shock and fever on his face. Fortunately, Michael is looking past him, into his bedroom. He has noticed the feathers. Slowly, with, it seems to Julian, impossible ease and casualness, he steps forward and kicks the door fully open.

'Yuck.' He says grimacing. 'What a mess!' He moves out of the way, and all at once the beautiful, sickening truth is revealed to Julian. There, on the carpet, lying on a modest death-bed scattering of its own feathers, is the bloodied, pitiful corpse of a pigeon.

'Will's got it in for you,' Michael remarks. 'This is like the horse's head scene in *The Godfather*. You'd better watch it!'

He notices that Julian is not sharing the joke, and spreads his hands in mock gravity. 'Hey bro,' he says solemnly, 'who died?'

Julian never knows what makes him do what he does next; all he can tell himself later is that whatever it was he was holding inside him had, at that moment, snapped, with all the force of a tortured piece of elastic. He feels himself quake, then he springs up suddenly and hits Michael hard round the face.

The next moment seems to be on freeze frame. Michael staggers slightly, staring at him in disbelief. He puts a hand slowly to his face. Julian stares back at him, breathing hard. An angry red swelling is forming on Michael's cheek, and his eyes are watering in pain. Then the world speeds up again. Michael steps forward and seems about to strike Julian, but then lets his hand drop. Wordlessly, he steps past Julian and out of the door.

Left alone, Julian sinks on to the floor beside the dead bird, seized with a strange feeling of *déjà-vu*. He is suddenly exhausted. He remembers when Michael had first turned up, that terrible night after he died when there seemed to be wailing coming out of nowhere, and every object in his room, from his intimidating black stereo system to the Peter Rabbit money-box he'd had since he was six, seemed to take up the scream. And then Michael had been there, and everything had been fine.

'Do you remember the moment you died?' Julian had asked later. 'Your whole life flashing before your eyes and all that?'

'Why would my whole life flash before my eyes?'

'I don't know. It's just what people say.'

'Have any of those people ever been dead?' Michael said. 'No, J, that's a load of crap. Don't remember a thing. Not a thing.'

Julian lies back on the floor next to the body that had once housed a spark, feeling part of a bizarre passing. He wonders where the pigeon's soul is. He closes his eyes. Before long, he sleeps.

When he wakes, stiffly and painfully some hours later, Michael is sitting on the end of the bed, his chin resting on his knees, his gaze straight ahead. Julian pulls himself slowly into a sitting position. Neither of them makes a sound; they just sit there, and for once their expressions are identical.

Eventually, Michael murmurs something into the stillness. He says it so quietly that Julian doesn't catch it at first and says, 'What?'

Michael says, 'I've really screwed you up, haven't I?' And he turns to his twin at last. Julian stares back. He nods. A heavy sense of finality oppresses the room.

Michael says, 'Simon's worried about you. Said so to Tom yesterday. Thinks you're acting weird.'

'What did Tom say?'

'What do you think? Didn't give a toss. But Simon says they've got to make sure you get out more.'

Julian nods. 'I like Simon.'

'Me too. He's a good friend. Oh yeah, and Sandra's shacked up with someone else.'

'Oh. Who?'

'Tom.'

'Oh.'

'Do you mind?'

'No.'

Michael slides off the bed and sits on the floor beside Julian. He says, 'You know, I just can't figure out what goes on inside your head sometimes. Never could.' There's a short silence, then Michael adds, softly, 'I don't think I'll stick around any longer.'

Julian turns to him and nods once, finally. 'Yeah.'

The next day, Michael walks to school with Julian for the last time. As they cross the street on to the pavement opposite their house, the journey they have done together so many times, Julian says, 'You could at least have picked a mildly credible way to die. What sort of idiot gets hit by a *micro-scooter*?'

'What sort of idiot *rides* a micro-scooter?' Michael rejoins. 'Who came up with them? Anyway, you're one to talk. What about the time you spent three days in hospital after running into a brick wall?'

'It wasn't a wall. It was a sort of partition.'

When they reach the corner before school, they both stop. After a brief pause, Michael proclaims, ' "All the world's a stage, and the men and women merely players. They have their exits and their entrances, and one man in his time plays many parts . . ." '

'What the hell's that supposed to mean?'

'No idea. Thought it sounded good in the circumstances.'

Julian shakes his head despairingly.

Michael says, 'I feel like I should say something profound. So Julian, I'm going to give you three pieces of advice: Firstly,' (with a wry smile) 'Always walk on the pavement. Secondly, "To thine own self be true"'. He pauses. 'And thirdly, in Shakespeare's words . . . Only wankers play the piano with their eyes closed.' They both grin. Michael grabs Julian's hand briefly. 'Take Mum up on her offer of cards. She could use it.'

Julian nods. Michael gives a small sigh. 'It was never going to be all right, was it?'

It is a rhetorical question. Julian says heavily, 'Bye, Mike. Take care,' which they both realise is woefully inadequate, and are simultaneously amused. They smile, mirroring each other perfectly. Then Julian turns and walks away, leaving his brother behind for ever.

Simon is waiting for him at the school gates. Julian doesn't look back. He knows Michael has gone. Michael is dead, and Julian understands at last, and grieves. But it is a new kind of sadness, of a much lighter kind than the load of suffocating misery he has carried throughout the last few months. Michael had recognised it before he had; and Michael had freed him. But what could that mean for Michael?

'You're looking contemplative,' Simon observes, 'for so early in the morning.'

'Well, you know how seriously I take school,' replies Julian absent-mindedly. Something has caught his eye. A feather. A white feather, fluttering slowly down in front of his face, and coming to rest at his feet. Marvelling at the coincidence, Julian bends down slowly and picks it up. A hint of the old spark glimmers in his eyes; Michael would have liked this.

'Come on, J, the bell's going,' Simon is saying. Julian pockets the feather. As they move away, he glances up briefly to see where it came from.

The sky is empty.

Haunted Holiday

Sahra Watkin

Haunted Holiday

I grumbled and groaned as I lifted my huge case up the stairs of the holiday cottage. My step-dad grinned. 'Need a hand?' he offered. I muttered something under my breath. I'd rather die than accept help from him. In fact, I thought, as I dumped my bag down for a quick rest, I didn't even know why I'd come on this dumb holiday. It was Wales, yes, and it was a pretty enough cottage, yes, but I couldn't help feeling like I had kind of traded in my mates for my step-dad. Now that was something I was *not* happy about.

I dragged my case into the bedroom I was staying in and looked around. It passed my judgement, but only just. I sighed as I noticed the two single beds. They were pushed close together. There was one thing I couldn't *stand* the thought of, and that was sleeping that close to my brat of a younger sister. I began to inch them apart.

Almost immediately my mum appeared in the doorway. 'What's that you're doing, Soph?' she asked, walking in (uninvited, I might add).

'What does it look like?' I mumbled, finally satisfied with the distance I had created. Mum sank down on to the nearest bed.

'It's such a shame you can't give your sister a

chance,' she moaned. 'She's twelve, after all, and you're fifteen. You should be able to be friends.'

I rolled my eyes. 'Mum, twelve is a totally annoying age. Even I was bad when I was twelve.'

She made a noise that sound like she was agreeing on this point. I thought that was a little unfair. 'But can't you just try?' she pleaded.

'I have, Mum, many a time.' I unzipped my case and began throwing things haphazardly into the wardrobe.

'Just once more? It would really make it a more pleasant holiday all round.' I knew that she meant for herself and Rob.

'OK, OK.' I caved in. Anything to get her off my back! I turned away, and started lining up my make-up products.

'Darling, really.' She came to stand beside me. 'I didn't bring even half as much stuff as this.' I shrugged and she finally took the hint. 'Well . . . I'll be downstairs if you need me.' She shuffled towards the door.

'Mum?'

She turned rather too quickly. 'Yes, sweetie?'

I gestured to the pictures on the walls. 'Why would you want such sad pictures up here?' She came back into the room and studied them. One was of a boy playing in the fields, the other was of a farmer in amongst his sheep, holding a rake.

'Well, Rodney's a farmer himself, isn't he?' she

said simply, as if that explained it. 'Now, call us if you need us!'

She headed off down the stairs. I looked out of the window and saw her helping to unload the car. I watched as Rob caught her in an embrace. It was quite sweet, really.

All of a sudden I felt a huge chill run through me. My bratty sister, Clara, had probably appeared and was watching me. She knew things like that scared me. However, as I turned, my eyes immediately landed on the picture of the farmer. Was he watching me? No, that was silly, I chastised myself. How could a person in a picture watch you? I looked over to the door, expecting to see Clara standing there, almost jumping with joy that she'd successfully scared me. She was nowhere to be seen.

That night we all sat in the small dining area with our fish and chips. The fire was crackling, although Rob felt the need to poke at it a little too often for my liking, and I was watching *Friends*, my most favourite show of all time. I was warm, happy and full. After I had eaten as much as I could manage I escaped off to the bathroom, showered and changed for bed. The shower was lousy but I wasn't in the mood for complaining.

'I'm off up to bed,' I announced to my mother.

'All right, goodnight darling.' My mother kissed me and Rob just sort of grunted.

I leapt up the stairs and bounced into the room,

and then I froze. Clara had moved the picture of the farmer. It was now facing the beds.

'Clara, you little brat!' I walked over to where the picture was. 'Why did you move this?'

Clara looked startled. 'Move what? That? I didn't touch him! He was there when I came up.' She returned to her book.

'Clara, it's not funny, you, know, trying to scare me like this. I know you were up here earlier, watching me.'

She looked up with interest. 'What is wrong with you, Soph? I wasn't up here; I was downstairs, playing with Rob!' A pang of doubt came over me.

'Really? Then how come this picture moved? Do you think pictures just move themselves?' I yelled. She looked confused, like she didn't know what question to answer first.

My mother came hurrying up the stairs. 'What's going on up here? You're making a racket!' She glanced at Clara's face. 'Sophie, are you upsetting your sister?'

I bit my lip. Of course, I had to be the one in the wrong.

'More like the other way round!' I exclaimed. 'That picture was above the beds right? And now it's here, and Clara won't even admit to moving it!'

My mother looked bemused. 'Clara, did you move the picture?' Clara shook her head. (Obviously.)

'She must have, Mum!'

My mother looked shocked. 'Honey, maybe it was there and you just can't remember.'

I paced the room. 'I know where it was, Mum! You're the one that can't remember, I showed it to you! Over there.'

My mother paused. 'I think we're all just tired and we're all getting mixed up.' She reached for the picture, and placed it on the hook above the beds.

'How come there are two hooks now?' Maybe I *was* tired.

'There now, girlies, be happy. I hear sleep calling.' She blew a kiss and switched the light out.

The darkness was so solid, I couldn't stand it.

'It's a bad omen to have a person hanging over the bed,' Clara whispered after a while. Her choice of words shocked me.

'What?' I hissed.

'The picture, you should've left him where he was happy.'

For a twelve-year-old that was pretty smart, but of course I didn't listen.

I slept fitfully that night. The farmer filled my dreams. He came towards me, his evil black eyes narrowed with anger. I could hear the church bells chiming twelve times in the background. Midnight. He was right up close on the last chime, his rake coming closer, closer. I tried to get away, but I couldn't move anywhere. I screamed, and then I woke up. Have you heard of that myth? People say that if you're falling in your dream and you don't wake up before you hit the ground, then you die. That's how near I felt to being caged in and killed.

It was, thankfully, morning when I awoke. I was drenched in sweat; and so was my bed. I crept downstairs before my mother could catch me (or smell me) and had a long, lukewarm bath.

'C'mon, lazy-pants.' Clara banged on the door, making me jump out of my skin.

'All right, all right,' I grumbled, pulling a towel around me and flinging open the door. 'Patience is a virtue, y'know.' I headed back upstairs.

'Did you have a bad dream?' Clara enquired. 'Mummy said she heard you scream. Was it that farmer?' She made ghost noises.

I threw a flannel at her and stomped up the remaining stairs. I began my usual morning ritual; deodorant, underwear, face, hair, clothes, all the time keeping my back to the picture, even though I could feel his gaze burning into my back.

'You want any breakfast, Soph?' my mother called. The smell of the bacon wafted up the stairs.

'Sure!' Anything to get out of this room. I could almost taste my mother's amazement; I hardly ever ate fried food. I turned and stared at the farmer. He had such an evil, dark, shadowy face. He glared evenly back. I wanted to throw something at him, but instead I glided calmly down the stairs to face the day.

The evening came all too quickly. We had spent the day looking round the town. It was actually quite fun. We'd had lunch out and then had gone for a long walk around some of the countryside. By the time we got back it had gone ten (we had dinner out too) and I felt exhausted.

'You don't want a bath?' my mother enquired.

'No, I'm just gonna hit the sack.'

She nodded. 'Sleep well.'

Clara was in bed before me again. The picture hadn't moved, but the room felt really cold.

'Clara, you open the window?' I asked sleepily, crawling into bed.

'Nope.'

I wrapped myself tightly inside my blanket and switched out the light.

Sleep came almost immediately. So did the farmer. It was the same as last time, but now I seemed to be in a cold, dark room. He hammered at the wooden door, battering it in with his rake. The church bells chimed again. I turned slowly in the room and felt someone else there, his breathing heavy. He lit a candle and I saw it was the boy from the other picture, the one in the fields. He looked lost, his mouth was moving but no sound was coming out. Suddenly, the farmer broke through, but instead of going for me he grabbed the boy by his neck and threw him against the wall. He turned to me.

'You'll be next,' he said. 'You'll be next.'

I woke up suddenly. Again, it was morning. I ran out of the room.

'Morning,' my mum chirped cheerily. 'Toast?'

I shook my head and gulped down some juice. 'There's something in that room,' I said quietly.

'Not that farmer business again,' my mother said.

'It's true. I've been having these dreams, these bad dreams.' I explained them briefly.

'Oh, darling, you're probably just finding it hard settling in.'

I kept quiet. I knew that wasn't it.

'Now, Rob and I are going out for a drive. Would it be OK If you looked after Clara for a couple of hours?'

How insensitive was that! 'Mum, I don't think that's a good idea.'

My mother giggled. 'Darling, there are fields for miles. What's going to happen?' She was already bustling around, tidying up.

'But that farmer . . .' I muttered.

'Stop that farmer business, too,' she said sharply. 'I don't want you scaring your sister.'

That was ironic. Me scaring her? Not likely. I was the one having all the bad dreams.

'Please,' my mother said, more softly. 'It will give us a chance to go and see what's around here.'

I almost laughed. Fields for miles, huh?

'Fine, I'll do it.'

Clara was happily colouring away at some picture of the Tweenies.

'Clara, I'm going to have a lie-down right?'

She looked up from her bed. 'That's not very responsible, is it?' she asked, apparently innocent.

'Well, if you want anything I'm right here.' I patted my bed. 'It'll only be for an hour or so. I just haven't been sleeping too well.'

She studied me intently. 'OK, Sophie, you sleep, I won't make too much noise.'

I smiled to myself. Sometimes she could be a real star.

The farmer was there to greet me as soon as I closed my eyes. He flashed into focus and then flitted out again, leaving only darkness. He filled that darkness suddenly, holding up his rake. I could hear somebody else's cries of terror in the background. The boy's, maybe? I ran forward bravely, calling out to him, but the farmer beat me off with his rake, leaving deep cuts on my hands.

'Sophie, Sophie, Sophie,' he said, with each slash. 'Sophie, Sophie!' The voice gradually turned into Clara's and I awoke.

'Some nightmare, Soph,' Clara said, leaning over me. 'Are you all right?'

I stood up shakily. 'This house is haunted.'

Clara's lip trembled and her eyes grew wide. I'd forgotten that she hated that word. 'Haunted? You mean like, g-ghosts?'

I rubbed my hands together, trying to inject some warmth into the rest of my body.

'Just two,' I answered, looking at the picture of the farmer. I suddenly grabbed it and threw it to the ground, smashing it to pieces. I reached in among the shards, cutting myself in the process, and took out the actual picture. I tore him into a thousand pieces and let them flutter to the ground. I could tell that I was scaring Clara but I didn't care. I had to do this.

I hurried downstairs, grabbed a carrier bag, flew back to the room and pushed everything into it, tying it tightly and shoving it into a corner.

'Sophie?' Clara sounded awestruck, somehow fearful.

'It's all right now,' I soothed, looking down at my hands. They reminded me of my nightmare. 'It's all right.'

My mother returned, all happy and upbeat. 'I thought maybe we could go to . . .' Her gaze fell in horror to my two bandaged hands. 'What happened?' She clasped them tightly and I winced.

'I dropped some glasses,' I said matter-of-factly. It wasn't the entire truth, but I had dropped three purposefully, just in case she chose to check.

'Darling, you should be more careful!' she tutted. 'Where's Clara?'

Clara ran down as if on cue. 'Here, Mummy.'

My mother rushed to her, and I saw her glance at her hands. 'Where you around when Sophie dropped the glasses? Did you hurt yourself?'

I saw Clara's puzzled look and I shot her a

warning glance. 'No, Mummy, but I heard them,' she said dutifully.

'Honey, try to be more careful!' she said to me again. It was always like this. Silly, silly Sophie, always wrong, always putting her sister in the face of danger, and clever Clara for keeping out of the way and being truthful. Yeah, right.

We went out for dinner again that night. It was hard for me to eat so I ordered small pieces of chicken and attempted to eat it with my bandaged hands, trying to ignore curious glances from the other diners. I dumped the bag full of the farmer in one of the recycling bins on the way back to the car park. Only Clara noticed; she gave me a meek smile. I had a feeling that she was hoping it would work as much as I did.

I rushed off to bed that night, frightened, but at the same time excited. Clara didn't say a word when I switched out the light almost as soon as I got under my sheets. I waited for what seemed like hours before I drifted into a peaceful sleep. The boy was there, but he was in a field instead of the darkened room. He was dancing, free and happy. On one of his twirls he caught me looking.

'Thank you,' he whispered, reaching for my hand. Mine was stone-cold but his was perfectly warm. We danced together, both of us knowing that the farmer would not return.

I woke up the next morning, when I could

reassure Clara that everything was very much all right.

The rest of the days flew by; a mixture of sunshine and sleep. On the last day my mother went to go and drop off the keys. As a matter of principle, I went too. The farmer was much older than I imagined, and a lot warmer than the one in the picture. His smile invited us in. While he and my mother chatted about her holiday, I looked in the kitchen. There were no creepy pictures, none at all, in fact. It was all over.

Well, not quite. I tuned into their conversation and realised that they were nearing the end. It was my turn.

'Um, excuse me, but I have something to say.'

He turned to me. 'Yes?' he asked kindly.

'There was a picture in my room, of a farmer,' I started. He nodded, understandingly. 'Well, when it was there I got lots of bad dreams and I couldn't stand it so I smashed it up.'

My mother gasped.

'And then?' the farmer urged, not looking a bit angry.

'And then it stopped – well, the bad dreams stopped, I still had dreams about the boy in the other picture, but not bad ones. It felt like he was glad the farmer was gone. He was happy and we danced.' I blushed at this last bit.

The farmer in front of me chuckled. 'Oh, dear girl, I don't doubt that your story's true. You don't seem the kind of girl to go around smashing things for the sake of it. And besides a few other guests have reported dreams similar to yours. None of them have been drastic enough to take action, though. I'm glad you did.'

I smiled. 'Still, I had no right, it was yours and I'm sorry. Here. This probably won't cover it but . . .' I held out a crisp twenty-pound note.

'Dear!' he protested, laughing. 'I bought that picture twenty years ago, and even then only paid about five pounds. You keep your money.'

I offered it again but he refused, so I slipped it into my pocket.

'Why was it so cheap?' I asked politely.

'Well, the old lady seemed very eager to get rid of it. She might've even given it to me for free if I'd tried hard enough. I'd never actually worked that one out, now you come to mention it. I really don't know.'

I smiled and turned to go, with the knowledge that at least one of us knew. I'm glad it was me.

If you would like more information about books available from Piccadilly Press and how to order them, please contact us at:

Piccadilly Press Ltd.
5 Castle Road
London
NW1 8PR

Tel: 020 7267 4492
Fax: 020 7267 4493

Feel free to visit our website at
www.piccadillypress.co.uk